SWEET TOOTH

SWEET TOOTH

YVES NAVARRE

Translation by Donald Watson

Dalkey Archive Press
Normal · London

Originally published in French as *Les Loukoums* by Editions Flammarion, 1973
Originally published in English by John Calder, 1976
Copyright © 1973 by Editions Flammarion
English translation copyright © 1976 by Donald Watson

First Dalkey Archive edition, 2006
All rights reserved

Library of Congress Cataloging-in-Publication available.
ISBN 1-56478-444-4

Partially funded by a grant from the Illinois Arts Council, a state agency.

Dalkey Archive Press is a nonprofit organization whose mission is
to promote international cultural understanding and provide a forum
for dialogue for the literary arts.

www.dalkeyarchive.com

Printed on permanent/durable acid-free paper, bound in the United States
of America, and distributed throughout North America and Europe.

For The sharp tooth, Douglas Cooper

Hell is on the level: without realising,
you walk straight into it.

Chapter One

I want to rip up the clouds. So thought Luc as the plane, throbbing and vibrant, lost itself in the stratosphere before finally rising closer to the sun, somewhere between our world and all the rest. In seven hours he would be in New York. Rasky's telegram had read: 'Meet me in New York City. Please. Rasky. P.S: I feel empty.' That was the old boy's style all right: he would go on to the bitter end acting like a spoilt child, like the possessor of so many playthings, which is how he looks on human beings, other people. But something in the form and tone of the telegram betrayed the anguish of a plea that was not this time due to caprice. Luc had realised that. In a world of make-up that so nearly fakes perfection, in a world of petty jet-set intellectuals, of lonely closet-queens salivating for the sweetness of soft-skinned youth, in this world of fascinating fascinated insects quivering at the merest flicker of desire, in this world which was his, sometimes words would trip you up, feelings would telescope. Suddenly a telegram could bear the seal of death. Luc would join the old boy again. He would be his last valet. It was the sort of task he was made for. And deep down it pleased him.

Rasky's first anxiety was whether Luc had met his house-keeper Odette all right. 'She explained it all, didn't she? Didn't forget anything? Watch out for the regulator on the shower it's the wrong way round. You might scald your-self. The air-conditioner in the library is out of action. The motor broke down the day before I left. In fact I've an idea that was really the cause of my departure: I began to swell up during the night. That's when my skin started to split. It's my skin that's killing me, you see.' Rasky lifted off the sheets and gently raised the dressings round his midriff. 'Look. It was the last thing I expected.' Luc approached the white bed. White ward, white sheets. 'Look at those little pink and red flowers all over my stomach: my blood. You can almost see what's going on inside. You don't feel like kissing me now, do you?' No trace of irony this time in Rasky's smile. And the voice had lost its edge, notoriously scratchy. Luc held out his hand. 'No, I wouldn't ask you that much. That's not why I sent for you. I just want to see you, at a respectable distance. I want to talk to you. And this time I want you to talk to me. I want you to tell me everything, all those things you never dared say before.' Silence. 'Sit down, Luc, over there.' Metal armchairs in white mock leather. Luc slid the chair over the marble-patterned floor. 'Yes; it's all white in here, like some funny sort of wedding. Perhaps they think that otherwise they might not find my sores. I'm going, Luc, I'm going. It's even more than I can do to raise my arm. I get the feeling it might drop off. So I keep still. They prop my head up. And I talk. Talk to you. I'm glad you're here.' Luc could hear the muffled scream of the town through the opaque glass of the blind picture window; he could hear the distant wail of the car sirens—police, fire and ambulance— and the throb of aircraft over Manhattan. 'You know, Rasky, in the plane I dreamt I was ripping up the clouds.' 'The clouds?'

    'I guess Odette told you you have to fasten all the locks in the apartment, even when you're inside. It's an essential precaution nowadays in this city. It's the least one can do.' Luc decided not to narrate his arrival at the airport. Ill-shaven and in blue jeans, he must have looked suspicious to the customs-officers. They had told him to open all his bags, including the plastic case for his typewriter. 'Pr-fession?' 'Journalist.' 'You here in New York on business or pleasure?' 'Pleasure.' Luc's voice quavers a little. Those eyes are threatening and he reacts like a guilty man. And

8

then the word 'pleasure' was loaded with irony. Luc barricades himself behind the ghost of a smile, which only makes his unhealthy stubbly face appear even more shady. They turn out his suitcase, an old suitcase more like a chest than anything else. 'You read too?' 'Yes, I read.' 'What?' 'I read what I like. 'And you like plenty?' The customs man pokes all round the sides of the case and summons one of his colleagues. They tap it, feel it all over, then pick up a knife, prise off the hinges and strip out the inside fittings, all that detailed workmanship once put into the making of luggage. 'But . . .' 'We know what we're doing.' 'But I care about that case.' 'And we care about our work.' Silence. 'I guess you know what goes on around here every day, don't you?' Other travellers are lining up behind Luc. They are motioned over to another check-point. Luc is sweating. Wipes his forehead with his hand and stammers out three words. 'But there's nothing . . .' 'That's what we're here to find out.' Silence. 'And what you've just said is just what you shouldn't have said. How many days you staying in New York?' 'I don't know . . .' 'You've gotta know that. How many?' 'Twenty . . .' Luc has just pronounced sentence on his friend Rasky. Or at least fixed an appointment for him with The Head Doctor, the Ultimate One who cures everything with a single stroke. Ah! And it wasn't for me to do that. 'It wasn't for me to do that.' 'Pardon me?' 'Nothing, I'm sorry.' The customs officers give up their search and replace all the fittings and bits of canvas they have torn out. 'O.K., you can pass. Here.' They hand Luc a scrap of pink paper which he holds in his outstretched hand for quite a while, just gazing into space: all his clothes lie scattered around his case and his travelling bag, hiding the typewriter from view. The customs officers turn their backs. Slowly and deliberately, Luc repacks his luggage: the city has rejected him. It was saying something like 'Get the hell out of here' or 'Get lost'. A few moments later Luc is hailing a taxi in front of the airport. Just as the driver is putting his bags in the trunk of the car, a man in blue comes up to him. 'Passport!' 'But I've just been through the customs.' 'Your passport! You know what this is?' asks the man, holding out a police-card. The cab driver shrugs his shoulders, unloads the baggage and disappears. 'What have I done wrong? I only wanted a taxi.' 'How long are you staying in New York?' 'Twenty days.' 'Business or pleasure?' 'Pleasure.' 'What kind?' 'Music. I like music.' 'What kind of music?' 'All kinds of music.' 'That's no answer.' 'But . . .' Give me a name!' Luc says nothing. 'You've forgotten.' Luc dips at random: '*Don Giovanni.*' 'O.K.' The man returns his pass-port and signals another cab. The city is rejecting Luc. In the taxi he feels like saying to the driver: 'Do you know what's just happened to me . . .' But he decides to keep quiet and lie low. Odette was waiting for him. He was late. The first thing she was to say was: 'Monsieur instructed me to tell you to make sure all the locks are fastened, even when you're inside the apartment. Lately he's been quite scared. Life has changed here now.' Rasky's life?

'What's on your mind?' asks Rasky. 'You aren't saying anything.' 'I don't like this room.' 'Would it surprise you if I told you that I don't like it either . . .' 'Sorry, Rasky.' 'Don't apologise. It's what I expected from you, now there'll be two of us to hate these three walls, this bed, that armchair and that opaque glass cutting me off from every thing. What's the weather like outside?' 'Humid, stormy, stifling.' 'What day is it? Tell me the date.' 'The twenty-eighth of September.' 'The twenty-eighth . . . you've just had your birthday?' 'The day before yesterday.' 'The first time I ever saw you, I was thirty-two as well. I was walking past the Lycée just as you came out.' 'You were cruising.' 'Right, I was cruising. And on the spot I offered to take you to *La Guerre de Troie n'aura pas lieu.*' 'And I accepted, on the spot.'

With every trip New York looks smaller and dirtier. With every trip, in Luc's mind, New York has sunk a little deeper, the skyscrapers seem more plausible and the giddy heights less outlandish. Either New York is subsiding into the polluted waters of the Hudson, or it is Luc riding high on one of his usual flights of fancy: and that is always the way with curiosity of all kinds. Time wears down the few soft edges of one's nature. 'What's on your mind?' asked Rasky. 'Speak to me . . .'

Half of Rasky's bed is like a tent: a metal bed-cradle supports the sheets above his legs. 'I can't walk any more. I dozed off on the sofa in the library. The air-conditioning went off. When I woke, impossible to get up. I was all swollen. Couldn't feel my legs any more. Odette had to call the doctor. When he arrived, complete with goatee beard, he didn't seem at all surprised. Just to console me, he said it ought to have happened before, much sooner. And I think it *was* some consolation. Now I don't give a damn, it's my heart, a matter of days. In fact, it isn't syphilis that kills you, is it? No, don't come any nearer.' Silence. 'Some folk go stark raving mad and hard as nails.' Silence. 'I'm just the opposite, as usual. Extremely lucid and soft as butter.' Silence.

Luc is taking leave of the editor of his magazine. 'I'm off to New York for three weeks. Here's my copy for the next three issues. I'll post the fourth one from over there.' 'What are you going for? Series of articles or a one-off report?' 'No, my good deed for the year. It's the boy-scout side of me coming out.' 'It'll be a waste of time, I'm sure.' 'No, I'll make something of it.' If life was no more than a tale of mystery, Luc would disapprove and find it all too obvious. But the course of life is never preconceived, anticipation is overtaken by events. Luc finds cold comfort in life's compositions. Not possessing the facile structures of story-telling, faked-up inventions nothing more, life skims the surface of things, scooping up casual comments,

11

whispered secrets of no apparent significance, feelings that are ephemeral, and only delves more deeply on those rare occasions when suddenly the heart-strings tighten. Then only one finds magic and emotion. Life takes chances. Life is a text each one of us interprets for himself. 'You'll never change,' the editor had said, as he pinched Luc on the cheek.

September in New York. The Indian summer was late. The city was only just emerging from the dog days, sweating, oozing humidity, black slime and grime. September in New York, with all the tourists transporting heroin in their baggage. Self-evident. It must seem a strange name to those customs-inspectors of despair: heroin(e)! Aren't the days of adventure long past, dead and gone? Yet all the passports of those ill-shaven blue-jeaned Parisian ladymen are phoney. Come on now, tell us the truth. Once out in the street and you are suspect. The clock has struck for playtime. Odette is handing Luc the keys. 'I'll be coming in just once a week, on Tuesdays. Monsieur told me you didn't like to be disturbed. And don't forget to tell Monsieur how sad I am not to be able to visit him. You'll go and sit with him instead. Tell him I'm expecting him. That he'll soon be back.' 'He won't, Odette, you know quite well he won't.'

Luc is taking a bath, even before he has unpacked his bags and hung his clothes up next to Rasky's: Rasky, the idol of the *salons*, that temperamental perfidious playboy of the summer of '39, the man who has always proved right. Luc is taking a bath. And he is back in one of New York's tiled bathrooms again with those damp gaps between the tiles, secret openings that lead into the subterranean labyrinth of the insect-world, earwigs and woodlice, beetles and scurbius, an inconceivably varied collection, the nocturnal denizens of the city's walls, a black-armoured host, gleaming black stones of ill-omen, stubbornly pursuing their mapped-out route across the tiling, indifferent to each other when the path of one insect happens to cross another's: blind. Luc will soon be paying Rasky his first visit. 'We can't even reach him by telephone you know, it's more than he can do to lift his arm. He's expecting you. Don't be late, Monsieur Luc.' 'I want to take a bath first and have a shave.' 'Don't be long.' How many million inhabitants are there in New York, how many million humans and how many billions of insects? Every wall is a continent. And it is their home, Luc is simply a guest. How many times has Rasky changed apartments, never daring to admit that he really wanted wholesome new walls and impeccable tiling in a clean shimmering bathroom: he was running away from the insects. But the insects soon began to invade the walls and take over their new domain. 'All my houses become coffins. Soon, too soon. I hardly have time to settle in, to get used to them. Creepy-crawlies are nibbling New York away.' His first bath: the insects have heard the water running. They go a bit wild. Come and inspect this friend of the master of the house, or come and listen to him rather, welcome him, threaten him. It's a *paseo* of sham indifference. Luc closes his eyes. The insects are there.

'As my friends can't telephone, they write. Rasky's going, they tell themselves, we must hail the farewell performance of the star queen.' Silence. 'Look on the bedside table, at that diamond fixed to the card with a strip of sellotape. From Anthony. He's an invalid too, at home in Venice. He assures me we'll both make a come-back at the drag balls before New Year's Eve and that we'll dance a waltz together. Why a diamond? Not long after the war he couldn't officially take money out of England to restore his little palazzo on the Grand Canal. He asked me to travel with him. Just near the frontier we stopped at a *café-tabac*: *pastis*, billiards and games of *belote*. Off he goes to the men's room and hides a little bag of diamonds in a place no customs-officer would dare to look. I remember it was

13

a village just beyond Chambéry. He was in there such a long time, I got quite worried. Later on, as he drove his Bentley over the Mont-Cenis pass, at every bend in the road you could see by his face he was in agony. I couldn't help laughing. Nor could he. And you see, he hasn't forgotten. One diamond! Well, it's yours. It's not worth much, it's probably flawed, but it will pay for your trip, or for your steam-baths anyway. You will be going, won't you? There's a brand new one on First Avenue, all fresh and clean. When you leave here, you should go. You can tell me all about it . . .' Insect. Silence. 'And then I had a letter from Pussysick. His antique shop is doing fine. You know that drag-queen. When a butch type wants to make love to him, he shakes his head, puts one hand over his frontal organ, with a pout says his Pussy is sick, and then points to the other one, the unexpected cross-functional one at the rear. He says in his letter that no-one else calls him Pussysick but me, that he can't think why and he'll miss me if I die. Charming! You see how spoilt I am by all their long letters. I'm finding out the way my friends write, their spelling mistakes and how they smudge their words when they're not too sure of their grammar. Seeing them as they really are, in fact . . .' Silence. 'And all these New York society ladies keep inviting me to the dinner parties they throw for their ladymen. Jewels and necklaces and daisy-chains of perfumed old fairies. At least I never used perfume. I always liked the smell of my own skin. A touch of pepper overlaid with a hint of sugar. The souvenir of a Turkish Grandma and a Rumanian Papa. But in fact you know nothing about my childhood, I must tell you . . .' Silence. 'Could you fold my hands over my tummy? That's it. Thank you.' A white silence. White marble-style floor. A scrape from the chair. Luc stands up and goes over to the picture window. 'It's no good. You won't see a thing. I'm nowhere in particular any more. I'm in a goods van going God knows where. But I'm already

14

en route. I never knew what it meant before, a one-way ticket. Oh, that hurts. Pull the pillow up at the back of my neck. That's it. Thanks.' Silence. 'And still they send me their invitations! I hate these fag-hag hostesses of New York, with their perfect dinners, all chichi and ribbons, with everything in pink or in blue. You go home with a pocketful of little gadgets, a personalized matchbox inscribed with I-love-you, or a table-mat with an embroidered wish to Forget-me-not. Too clever by half. And the dishes, all those sauces and cream things and fluffy bits and pieces, and all those people expecting a bitchy wisecrack from you, like "Oh, so you're Swiss! I love, I adore Switzerland. The taste of boredom there is quite unique." And they laugh. And I listen to them laughing. Then they say I'm a hopeless case. Damned right they are. So I close my eyes, and I don't care *that* for them.' Silence. 'When my socks fall down, I pull them up. And they stare at me. It's not done, is it, to pull your socks up in front of everyone, after dinner in a smart drawing-room in a penthouse, 812, Fifth Avenue. Then I admit . . . that I just find it hard to make them laugh when my socks are falling down. And off they go again. I amuse them. They're still laughing at me today: and I'm going to die. They're pleased as Punch. I still amuse them, you see.' Silence. Luc gets a vague impression of the city in outline, the glow of the setting sun and the soft touch of the clouds as they melt away, subtly tinting the sunset. A fuzzy picture postcard. The wail of ambulances and police patrol-cars. 'They call me a crank, keeping identical apartments in London, Paris and New York, and insisting on the same bed in each of them, same furniture, same books, and the same records. But there's one thing in New York that Paris and London don't have, and that's walls, all that life going on in the walls. The insects are back again, you noticed.' 'Yes, I noticed.'

'He was a doll. I met him at Uncle Bernie's, at the bar. He was thirty. He was German. I don't know why I think

15

of him in the imperfect. Because there was no hope of sex with him, I suppose: he found me repulsive. But he wanted to talk. Me too, so I invite him back to my place. He's from Berlin. Thirty. With no ulterior motive, he says he finds the apartment too hot. The air-conditioning in the library had broken down, so now you know this all happened a week ago. He asks if I mind him removing his shirt. He is smothered in scars, all over his stomach, his back and his arms, furrowed with them. I ask him if he wasn't in Amsterdam about twelve years ago? He tells me he was. At Easter? Yes. One day, in front of the Rijksmuseum, late in the afternoon, did you meet someone who took you back to a room in the American Hotel? Yes. That was me! And the young man's astounded to be suddenly recognised like that. But how? I am caressing his old wounds. When I'd made love to him in Amsterdam, we did everything. A skin-bag of scars. It was frightful. But I'm a courteous man, as you know.' Silence. 'The young man left and I fell asleep on the sofa. And now you see, I find myself in here. With my smooth skin swelling and splitting. I'd be delighted to be smothered in scars. I'm not breaking up, I'm just bursting out all over. And there's nothing anyone can do. So there you are. That was my last trick. I think his name was Martin.' Silence. 'You go off to the steam-baths now. Yes, go for my sake. Go on. Don't forget Anthony's diamond and Pussysick's address: I'd like you to answer his letter. Tell him I've come to a sticky end. Sticky, yes that's it. Off you go then, it's time. Come again tomorrow at five, won't you? Without fail.' Silence. 'No, don't kiss me.'

Chapter Two

113 Central Park South, seventeenth floor, Veronese Suite:
Lucy Balsam is not too sure what she came to New York
to do. Well, perhaps she is: and she's waiting. It's always
being told, the tale of two people who meet and then make,
unmake and break their relationship, that eternal last page
in every story about an average couple. But whatever it
was that happened to each one of them beforehand is never
or only rarely recounted. It was a book Lucy Balsam
would have loved to write! Lucy Balsam would have loved
to *write*! The trouble is, she's bored. She wishes the phone
would ring a bit more often at night, like this: that's
someone! Hello! Lucy Balsam imagines a double story, a
plan for a novel of parallel lives: two characters before
they meet. Something wrong: their destinies can hardly
run parallel, since they are going to meet! Lucy Balsam
smiles. All her projects fill her with emotional anxiety. She
accepts her dreamed-up fantasies like a little girl receiving
a little doll—at last: late in the day, very late, far too late
for her to play with it. Lucy Balsam is nearly fifty years old.
Still beautiful. That she knows. She is not yet afraid of
mirrors. And at night, all it needs is one simple gesture to
pick up the telephone, and Jack would fix her an appointment in one of his establishments between West 80 and
West 90, where there are so many handsome Puerto
Ricans, at times very young and sweet. The only snag is
that Lucy Balsam wants the appointment all to herself.
And Jack has more and more customers, and Jack wants
more and more money. Lucy Balsam imagines a novel
which would not reveal all from the start. And that was
surely the reason why she had never written one herself.

She would get launched in a few lines and give the whole game away, tell everything about everyone, in short, anticipate the end of her little tale, screwing her handkerchief up with impatience, to find herself all too soon intimidated by a still incomplete first page in which everything was already near completion. She would smile, rip out the offending page and then call up Kenneth, the bellboy in the block, to ask him to order a car. Today perhaps she would go for a walk in Central Park. Go and watch the squirrels and the colourful little old ladies sitting on the benches in the sunshine. She would stroll along, dressed in grey as if in mourning, haughty and remote, hiding behind sunglasses so as to be quite sure that she would not pass unnoticed. Her hired chauffeur would follow at a distance, either to make an impression or else in fear lest someone should attack her. You never can tell. The London newspapers reported that Central Park was dangerous again, even in broad daylight. And Lucy Balsam, née Lucienne Roussel, a native of Carpentras with a mania for New York, but a Londoner at heart and by adoption, takes the English journalists at their word. Not the others. In New York she never reads the papers anyway. She goes there because at times Jack calls her up. Jack, the gentleman at whose place the destinies of all who figure in her little world cease to run parallel. Lucy Balsam decides to be patient for another two or three weeks. The sun is setting, a few stray wisps of cloud cling to the skyscrapers on Fifth Avenue. One of them makes a pretty little veil round the Hotel Pierre. Lucy Balsam will take a bath and go to bed very early. Perhaps Jack will call her during the evening. Perhaps, just perhaps.

An all-grey lady in an all-green apartment. A sad-looking lady, but who still knows how to smile at the thought of all those things she might have done in life and all that she has failed to do. To write, if only she had learnt how to write! If only she had learnt, just for once at least, how to dampen her enthusiasm in the first few pages of a novel, how to keep the secret of her book to herself and not blurt it out before the final chapter, when the reader, that intimate and distant friend, can contain his miraculously heightened curiosity no longer and is waiting all agog for one thing only: the revelation of some name or place or magic phrase which will crack for him the enigma of some-one else's life and all those aspirations upon which his own have been projected. Oh, to become a great lady novelist!

Veronese Suite, what a name for the haunt of a wealthy winsome widow, who has grown strict and sensible in her extravagance. Barnaby Balsam, the Great B.B. of London's High Society between the wars, had left his beloved Lucy enough to keep her well-provided with furs and jewels till the end of her days, till the end of the century if she were to last that long. Lucy smiles. All very fine, those furs and jewels, for a young girl from Carpentras, the little bilingual secretary and shorthand-typist who was the darling of all the local ladies. 'She'll go a long way, your daughter, Madame Roussel. And pretty with it!'

Lucy thinks: 'I'd have been quite happy, writing myself to death. I wonder why? Who or what would I have been afraid of then? Of myself? Night has come now. Perhaps Jack has forgotten me. Or does he keep me waiting on purpose? Or is it because he knows how fussy I am? Did I appear too hard to please at my last rendezvous? Courtly love has gone for ever. Ah! I ought to note that down. It would make a good opening page for that novel I can't give birth to. A Caesarean. There I go, smiling again. I hate smiling. It gives me away: I'm out of tune with myself. I wonder what time it is in London now? Paul and Mary will be having dinner in the butler's parlour. Talking about me, wondering what I'm getting up to all alone in New York. She'll go a long way, little Lucy, she'll go to New York.'

Who was it had said to Lucy: 'I'd rather see a lady turn secretary than a secretary turn lady. It's too common-place, not so amusing. When women like that make the grade, they lose whatever was going for them before when they were fresh and pretty, appetisingly gauche and positively charming in their gaucherie. And they never completely master their new role. Life makes them disguise themselves, they're walking ghosts, well-dressed and well made-up, with an eternal Touch of Youth, ageless. They bury their beneficent husbands and then these winsome widows await the final act, which never comes, Act Fourteen, Fifteen, Sixteen: a secretary turned lady is a one-woman-show that goes on and on for ever. Death takes a willful revenge by arriving late in the wings. It's her style of punishment.' And Lucy smiles: that is how she would define herself in a novel, if she had to define herself. But to hell with that idea. Over her face Lucy fixes the satin mask that blinds her, she pulls the night down over her face. 'You have the loveliest wrinkles, Madam, you mustn't fight them, you must cherish them.'

Lucy Balsam is in love with death. And why not. On the bedside table next to her fur-covered bed stand the telephone (for Jack), a photograph of Barnaby (the thirteenth of July 19.., Antibes, one hour later he made a stupid fall between two yachts and had his head crushed between the two hulls, why should a silly accident like that make one feel guilty, it's always the same old story) and a photograph of Lammert (it was when he was thirty, a year ago already, taken on his thirtieth birthday, just before he flew to Lusaka, his first embassy posting, smiling as he got out of the taxi at Schipol Airport, Amsterdam, and it was Lucy who took the picture. Next time she saw him, at Lusaka, he was dead. Another airport: Lammert was on his way to welcome Lucy when his car had swerved and burst into flames. Lammert's body could hardly be distinguished from the charred remains of the car. Lucy did not even have the strength to weep.)

20

Courtly love has gone for ever: burnt out. Romance with an R has gone for ever. A mere lying pretence on the part of those who are trying to flout death. And Lucy is in love with death, the rival who has just robbed her of Lammert, a dream-lover in the mind of a young girl from Carpentras. And Lammert was sincere when he took her in his arms. Their mad passion was eminently sensible. Lammert made love with his eyes wide open. He gave himself. Ten months ago at Lusaka, one episode ended and another began. Lucy was ready to admit that she had reached an age when one look alone was not enough to launch a conversation. For one moment, when she was well on her way through life, Lammert had distracted her from that corrosive thought. She had been caught up in Barnaby Balsam's career in the days of his splendour. 'You're our little Mademoiselle from Carpentras,' he used to say, 'and that's far more exciting than a little Mademoiselle from Paris. It's far more unusual anyway.' And she was to get caught up in Lammert's career in the days of *his* splendour. 'You'll always have the legs of a girl of twenty, and you'll always have fabulous breasts . . .' But who was that talking? Was it they? They are there all right. Hidden in the fur.

Night falls, with the mask, over Lucy's face. Jack will call her, tomorrow or the day after. Lucy bites hard on her lips: she does not want to kid herself with promises or fall into the snare of her own reassurances. Her mask is the night, an apprenticeship for death. Are you there, Lammert? Seventeenth floor, Veronese Suite, 113 Central Park South, New York City. I'm alone and I'm waiting for you. Ten months without you is far too long.

Chapter Three

'I'd like to see what's going on behind those tiles.' Sauna
Bath Unic, First Avenue, between 2nd Street and 3rd
Street: the new Sauna popular with clients in search of
something fresh, arse-fresh. Luc has gone to lie down near
the pool in the basement of this mansion of love, with its
soft music, discreet perfumes and individual cubicles, with
clean sheets, bars of soap and anal ointments in the drawer
below the ash-tray. The imbibing of alcohol and the use of
drugs are forbidden. 23.30: Luc watches the queens of the
night to-ing and fro-ing as they make their little deals in
the showers and the steam-room. Luc watches the divine
young things daintily dip in the pool as they let out delightful little shrieks. White, black and chocolate, 'les girls' of
New York in quest of a few palpitating moments in one
another's arms. But the twitter of these ladies is colourless,
a ballad of white tiling and grey marble where glowing
spotlights stroke the walls of that great foyer of aimless
encounters. Bitchy remark overheard: 'When Sills sang
Lucia at the City Opera, the orchestra quit playing and she
just carried right on. In the mad scene she went on singing
five minutes after they'd all stopped. Can you imagine? She
belts out a top E when it should be a C sharp. And she gets
away with it: she's the Queen of the City Opera'. Luc
listens and registers. Tomorrow he'll tell Rasky all about it,
up there in that other white coffin, in Sutton Hospital.
    A scurbius: Luc recognised it by its hundred velvety legs
and its purplish wings. The light from the spots made its
carapace shine. It sidled along the wall, disappeared
behind a chrome fitting, then re-emerged with its mates:
the scurbius in procession, one, two, three, and then four,

and five, they have found an ideal hunting-ground, a scrap of discarded food, a bit of soap, or else some chewing-gum spat out by a bad-tempered fairy, furious at the time she has wasted looking for a man to roll her on the bed of her cubicle upstairs, on the second, third or fourth floor, which has a different procession of different scurbius each with a gleaming carapace of a different hue. 'The management requests that their clients on the upper floors keep the noise level down so as not to attract too much attention.' When you make love, grit your teeth. Luc closes his eyes. That is his last word. What copy can he find to send his editor from New York, if by any chance Rasky lingers on and postpones his final departure? The Scandal of the Marble Halls? The death of a terminal syphilitic whose life is seeping away and who, with the remaining sparks of youth, boldly flashes his astonished eyes at you, as you abandon him to the last bedroom he will know, a luxury lab for a luxurious gentleman falling apart at the seams? 'But Doctor, his skin's giving out!' 'It's what I expected.'

Luc has some farewell letters from Rasky in his baggage. A sort of summary of a messed-up affair. A gentleman in love with a young man. A young man out of love with his own times. A gentleman with too much money. A young man who refused to take any more of his parents' money. Who wanted to be independent. To earn his own living and indulge his curiosity about all that went on around him, especially life itself. The gentleman starts courting the young man. He is a courteous gentleman who dreams of courtly love. He decides to play fair by the young man and warns him: he is syphilitic but he is not contagious. He has been treated, the disease has been halted. He has regular check-ups. He probably caught 'it' in 1939 from a gigolo passing through Paris. 'He was beautiful, I don't blame it on him. Only I caught the disease in a place where it's totally hidden. And that was that. When I found out, too late, seven years later, it could only be held in check, to stop Dame Syphy nibbling me away. You see, I'm warning you. I've never confessed this to anyone before. It's something that's never mentioned, is it? Besides, it's always other people who catch it.' Only too well Luc recalls when the gentleman gave his secrets away: it was after *La guerre de Troie n'aura pas lieu*. And then the war *did* take place. The schoolboy had a high old time with the gentleman. Because the gentleman was nice-looking, kind and frank. Because he offered him all the things he could have done without. Luc came to life.

Farewell letter No. 7.

'Dear Luc Damesieur, You're asking for a slap in the face, Ladyboy. Or a good hiding. Your face being where your arse ought to be. Your intelligence doesn't outstrip the hypersensitivity you so carefully camouflage, so you fail in your pursuit of one of the standard goals in life: happiness. The day I see you looking blithe and gay as a Dresden shepherdess, I shall be God the Father God the Son. But I can hear your footsteps on the stairs and I intend to throw you out. So much honesty stands between us, it's quite unbearable. And the eyes of a college boy . . . (when on earth are you going to stop telling me about your practicals, your essays, your Part I's and Part II's, what are all these 'Parts' anyway?) . . . those college boy eyes tell me only too clearly what I am. I shall hand you this note. I'm writing it in haste, in memory of you. And it amuses me to close this letter of dismissal without endearments. Rasky.'

Farewell letter No. 23.

'Dear little Luc, You make me feel so much older than you and so much less attractive that you fill me with complexes. Yet you appear to enjoy my caresses. And I can hardly say I'm displeased by the way you look at me—surprised and happy, it seems, when I lie down beside you

25

and cuddle up close. I'm leaving for London tomorrow, an unscheduled trip: we won't be meeting again for a while. Be so good as to return the keys of the lower locks to the concierge. To be on the safe side, I'm keeping the third one locked, the one at the top. In spite of what I told you, I haven't lost the third key. Don't accuse me of being bloody-minded, it's just commendable caution. I know you're going to pass your *Bachot*, so I congratulate you in advance. I'm leaving, so I kiss you goodbye. There was something under the surface that kept us apart, a certain Dame perhaps. A secret we shared. So by being frank, you see, I got caught in my own trap. I'm leaving and I kiss you goodbye. Rasky.'

Farewell Letter No. 43.

'Luc, you're a male *grande dame*, with reasons for her behaviour that reason barely comprehends. Let me explain: the mist-trails of early morning lack the fresh aroma of rosy-fingered dawn, they already smell of that smoking Jet roaring off to Fiumicino, ready to throw you into someone else's arms, one of our friends, who knows? You see, I know it all. Nelson has invited you to spend a few days with him. That's fine. He's so delightful! The way you lit your cigarette this morning as soon as we woke, after favouring me with a night in your garret room, and then the nervous way you smoked, even before you'd made a cup of that bitter coffee you alone know how to concoct, put me wise to this departure of yours, which you have concealed from me, which *you* have provoked . . . and *I* wished for. This time it is you pulling away from me. And I feel sure we shall never see each other again. This is my last letter. I love you. The closer I come to you and the harder I try to understand your smiles, the more embroiled I get in ridiculous attempts to tack up all those evening gowns which we shall never wear, condemned as we are to be content with our own sex. But I'm digressing. You take

26

jam with your breakfast in order to sweeten that laugh of yours, which would have made Dr. Charcot call you 'a hopeful case . . . '. Like a budding flower of civilized sensibility, you do still make an engaging if disquieting impression, which owes less to your smile than to the silence that ensues. But when a flower starts blaspheming, the will-o-the-wisp runs riot through the night, stirring up ghosts, releasing spirits from bodily restraint. I call a halt. I take flight, afraid I might meet you on the service stairs. You have gone to say hello to your parents. You see, you still belong to them. So you are the one person I shall never be able to buy. I shall never own you. Enjoy the hot croissants of our last breakfast all by yourself. Keep yourself company by looking at your own smile in the mirror over the wash-basin. Then perhaps you'll understand what you were trying to tell me. Perhaps you'll find out at last in what direction you really want to go. Goodbye. Your body was a great comfort to me. I shall play around with other people's 'in the attempt to find you again'. And I sign off with: your hope-less daddy. P.S. I was foolish enough to re-read what I've written. What Charcot would have said was not a hopeful case . . . but a hopeless one. Your smile is a mirror of me. Intolerable. There are three of us. We are both sitting on Dame Syphy's knees. We are her twin sons. But I am my mother's boy. Not you. You.'

Farewell letter No. 77.

'My Luc. The number 8 is the figure of death. Have just read in Van Gogh's Letters dated 8th September 1888 the following words, which you ought to take to heart: 'how does one get through this wall? It is no good battering against it. In my view one has to whittle it down and file one's way through slowly and patiently.' I have been accused of not lifting a finger all my life except to sign cheques and count banknotes, buying other people's time

27

and forgetful of my own. This constant implacable prison, which is only too familiar, is always with me wherever I am; I have decided to go back inside again, just when through you I thought I would be leaving it for good. It's a cosy refuge when I feel threatened, a haven of vertical walls, all breached in my fruitless attempts to escape. I shall be back where I belong, a schizoid Jack-in-the-box, alone apart from Dame Syphy and the lordly Tests of Nelson, her aristocratic cousins, you know the ones, unmentionable at fashionable parties where snooty pretty-boys keep ostentatiously quiet about the life they lead in the suburbs. Thank you for smiling. And thank your smile for showing me the way back to prison again. That's at least one good thing you will have done in your life. I've made up a bag of the odds and ends you kept at my place, either out of habit or in case you got stranded once more. I offered you everything, gave you every opportunity: yet you never really made yourself at home. Paper money, that's all I have to give you. And you won't even take that. Monsieur plays at being one of those splendid students who are out to make a new world. Hail and farewell, bright star: I shall inscribe your name on the walls of my jail. And Dame Syphy, who never got her hands on you, will give me a playful pinch in the arm. Rasky.'

Postcard.
  'You are just a smiling bastard. Rasky.'

Farewell letter No. 113.
  'You can have too much of a good thing. Like too much sweetness, too much silence, too much nice fresh milk. Greedy puss: it's all too much. Remove all these excesses from your life and we shall meet again, a sorry couple perhaps, but a nice agreeable pair. *Ciao Bello*. I'm going to see if you're not to be found in the steam-baths of New York. But you won't be. Thank God.'

28

Farewell letter No. 173.

'The tenth anniversary of our first meeting. You're not coming out of school any more, now you've gone into journalism. Your new daddy edits a political journal. Political? In France? Have you taken up the art of slippers and a pipe? Who are you rooting for? My dear Luc, I know you save all my letters to build up a collection. Farewell letters you call them. Not farewell, just fare-well. They signal our continuity, not our rifts. How could I cut myself off from you now? The further I go from you, the more I love you: keeping at a distance is the finest proof of our affection for each other. And you, handsome smiler, that's exactly what you want. Say it, admit it, just once. And write to me, just once. No, you're smiling. I come back, and you smile. Till we meet again, very soon, your friend Rasky.'

Farewell letter No. 201.

'Here I am sacrificing another letter in the ritual of Lucan farewells. The French have a taste for quotations: they always seek refuge under someone else's roof when obeying the little dictates of their conscience. In one of Sartre's pieces, about Mallarmé, I came across the following remark: "time no doubt is an illusion: in men's eyes, the future is just an aberrant aspect of the past." It is by studying the way other people treat your body and the use you make of your own smiles and silences—which might pass for foolish provocation, though it is far from that— that you screw up the courage to go scouting for the truth about our loneliness and our cowardly reluctance to accept fulfillment. Curiosity is right at the bottom of my strong-box, underneath the title-deeds and the cash. I only take it out when there's nothing else inside. And you are the only one who leaves me skint. Isn't that the nicest confession I've ever made to you? I ask you to live with me and you won't. I offer you everything and you want nothing. You retort that you can't go along with this feeling I have, that someone who has everything has nothing. You want to remain a scribbler, recording the society of our times, an age which isn't one, a period you blush and grieve for when you realise it's your own. You want to contemplate your country and study its withdrawal to the balcony of history, remote and safely ensconced, self-righteous and superciliously determined to ignore whatever confrontations the future holds in store, accepting only what bolsters its security. It's the country for a fireside snooze, isn't it? Wasn't that one of your expressions? In offering myself a nice discreet companion, a rival to Dame Syphy, someone to read my farewell letters, I never thought I ran the risk of saying farewell to myself. My future is just an aberrant aspect of the past in the eyes of a man like me, checkmated, possessed, polluted and apparently polite, attractive still, who knows, or do you deceive me when you open out your arms? And here I am, a man worn down by habit, thanks to you. A man who has got used to having nothing. And Nothing gives a sense of order. Forgive me for being difficult if I ask you not to call me up again. Or even phone Chris or Maria, who definitely see you as my saviour. Besides I do not intend to run for safety to London or New York. I shall take a little trip elsewhere, all alone, alone at last with my load of introspection, submitting myself to endless customs examinations as I rummage through my despair, with surplus luggage to be paid for each day out of my own heart's blood. Splattt! Customs check. I'm digressing, aren't I? And if I were to ask you not to write, would you write to me, just once at any rate? I embrace you. With affection. But don't let my affection quicken one of your smiles. I hope you can remain impassive for the brief time it takes to confide a secret, like the one in this letter for example. I shall know when the moment comes. And for at least one moment in my life I will not have been alone. Once more I embrace you. I am writing this to the memory of you. Our life in a sheaf of pages. A perfect souvenir. If only these sheets could become the sheets on your bed . . .' Fifteen pages.

Farewell letter No. 297.

'My intangible friend, Luc. I was watching you at that restaurant my friends took us to. We were six at table and I was afraid a seventh would come and take over: boredom. That is why I played the fool, while you with your silences seemed to be summoning the uninvited guest. You see what I mean? The clatter of that bead curtain, which separated us from the kitchen, each time one of the waitresses brushed it aside, was getting on my nerves. So to rid myself of irritation, I made a sardonic joke. I said, and I'm sure you remember: 'Oh, that bead curtain! Every time the waitresses go through it I feel as though I've lost a string of pearls." The others burst out laughing, but not you. Not because you didn't understand—you know perfectly well that I move in a fashionable set, quick to pick up any remark one drops—but because you had made up your mind to make me see myself as the foolish clown I am. So *I'm* dropping *you*. And all your life you'll get dropped: one can't go on constantly bringing people face to face with themselves. Today I detest your smile, it's a smile that leads me back to myself. At least leave me the comfort of living in comfort, with the privilege that money brings. I'm an old wolf in drag, a faggot if you like: was that what you tried to tell me by not laughing? I hope it won't be long before you're a worn-out threadbare old rug. Today I could strangle you. It goes without saying I've called off your trip to New York. So you won't get to see it after all. The spiteful say that my apartment there is the same as the other two in Paris and London. They're quite right: I don't live anywhere. So have no regrets. Tear up the airline ticket I gave you the day before yesterday. I trust you for that. Rasky.'

Farewell letter No. 313.

'Luc. I shall never forget, young man, the week-end you've just spent in my flat in London. What a hypocrite! I'm used to rubbing shoulders with all sorts of folk. I'm an old pro when it comes to taking pretty young things under my wing. Long before you were born I was jumping in and out of the arms of Viennese gigolos and Rumanian sailors. But though you came with no luggage, it took *you* just two days to turn my house upside down. You put me on bad terms with my friends and to cap it all Chris and Maria have stood up for you. I guess Odette would have done the same in New York: servants adore you. They don't breathe a word either. They just smile. Are you out to destroy me? Once and for all, forget that I exist. To think I've been singing this old refrain for twelve whole years! You're worse than a *femme fatale*, you're a proper young man all right. I felt far too good in your arms. Bravo and goodbye. Rasky.'

Visiting-card slipped under the door.

'You're like a film-star, a shooting star, zooming away . . . Rasky dropped by. You weren't in. Are you making love to your editor, your Roneo Romeo?'

Pre-farewell letter No. 357.

'Every year I get one year older. Every year you get one year younger. It's not fair. I don't know how you still find me attractive. If only you could close your eyes for once when you make love to me. The time has come for that now. The way you look at me, I can't face it any more. Please. Or don't let us ever meet again. Agreed? Rasky.'

Farewell letter No. 377.

'Own up, Luc! You were bored stiff last night. Well, I *like* music-hall, with its smell of rabbit fur and cheap cosmetics. I like its tawdriness. Those phoney sparklers open up new horizons for me. I enjoy all those pointless songs. They make me forget. With you there, however, I remember everything. And I regret what I'm doing and all that I did before. It wasn't a college boy I picked up outside that school, but a butcher with a satchel stuffed with knives. You get a kick out of giving me everything, don't you, and accepting nothing in return? Say it's true, admit it for once in your life. This express letter should make it quite clear that tonight's dinner is cancelled, and that I'd rather not see you again. For a time, anyway . . . Thanks. Rasky.'

Letter No. 413.

'Luc, my love, they're jeering at us. They've always jeered at us. They say you're destroying me. But what is destroying me is their jealousy. I should like to give you something, just once, tell me what? On second thoughts, no: I want to make a deal with you—and it's imperative you agree. As I said before, the finest proof of our affection for each other is to keep at a distance. Let us not see each other at least for a year. I'm leaving for New York. I'll write to you regularly. Call me whenever you like. The more often the better. But don't come over. Of if you do, don't tell me, don't show yourself. Give me a wide berth. If only I had given you a wide berth that day outside your school. It's all been too wonderful. Everything that has passed between us is too wonderful. I'm looking for the stage-door, for an actor's way-out. There are plenty of them in New York. This time it's serious. It's a deal that springs from affection, please accept it: *Merci*. Rasky. Mercy.'

Telegram. One year later.

'Meet me in New York City. Rasky. I feel empty.'

Chapter Four

The awakening of Goldilocks: Lucy tears off the silken mask that creates night for her. How many hours has she been asleep? How the hell can she sleep twelve hours in a row with no-one and nothing to aid her? What a way to waste time, my dear, when you're fifty years old! What a way to fill time when you've nothing, but nothing to do. 'While you lie in in the mornings, I'm out at work,' Lammert used to say as he stroked Lucy's hair. 'It's still beautiful, my hair, don't you think?' 'Why still?' They established an air-lift between Amsterdam and London Lucy joined Lammert in Amsterdam, Lammert joined Lucy in London. It was at the funeral of her husband Barnaby that Lucy first saw Lammert. 'He was my Professor in International Law, I was very fond of him.' 'I know, he told me about you, thank you for coming.' The accidental death of B.B. had been announced in the French newspapers. The Anglican Church in Nice was packed with stiff-necked sun-tanned Britishers, a fashionable circle of friends on holiday on the Riviera, snooty and correct. Lammert, holidaying in a village in Haute-Provence that had been taken over by the Dutch, had decided to come and pay his respects to his Professor. Besides, he could use the opportunity to go bathing. That summer was so scorching it took you by the throat. He waited while everyone filed past, wanting a quiet word with Lucy Balsam, to have his little say about the great Barnaby. He let the others go first: the starchy, hidebound English, then Cousine Elia and a few friends from Carpentras, a contingent of neighbours from the past life of Lucienne, now known as Lucy, all humble folk from her

35

childhood. 'If you finish your homework before supper, you have permission to use my chair and sit on the balcony for half an hour, I'll lend it to you.' *'Merci, maman.'* That chair spelt life, the street and people passing, the interminable approach of nightfall, the laughter and whispered secrets of folk who have chosen to live out their lives in Carpentras, and die there. The balcony was the airport of Lucy's dreams. 'I shall be an air hostess, no perhaps not, an executive secretary, and I'll fly round the world with my director.' 'Lucienne, you're dreaming, work!' *'Oui, maman.'* And in the evenings, before she went to bed, Lucienne would stroke her curly fair hair. Stroke her silky hair and imagine someone else's caress, imagine what a different hand from hers would think and feel as it ran all that softness through its fingers. 'I'm pretty, but that's not all I am', she would say to her looking-glass, an open book of fairy tales which contained but one: her own. She would go a long way. She promised herself. And when the war was over, when she'd taken her *Bachot*, she would go to Paris to her cousin Elia's and look for a job. Lammert was kissing her hand. 'He was my Professor in International Law, I was very fond of him. So . . .' 'I know, he told me about you, thank you for coming.' A good lie that. Lucy did not even know the young man's name. 'Do you mind if I take your arm? I don't feel much like talking to my cousin, still less to the Professor's friends. And they're waiting for me, you see. Do you mind walking me back to my car? Do you mind?' She had spoken very quickly, nervously, in a strained little voice. She was thinking about Barnaby, the way they had met, and the whole delightful story of the green dress she had worn that evening, of the continuity of her life. 'Barnaby arranged this meeting for us, didn't he?' 'I beg your pardon?' 'Oh, what a silly thing to say. Let me ask you to lunch. I've got nothing fixed for this afternoon. For afterwards. It's true, these last few days I'd almost forgotten that afterwards I wouldn't know

what to do or where to go.' 'To Carpentras?' 'I daren't.'
'To London?' 'It'll rain right through the summer.' Lucy
acknowledged her friends, oh just a few little waves of the
hand, discreet black-gloved salutations. 'No-one but the
friends we always tried to avoid.' 'I beg your pardon?'
'I've lost my voice, don't mind me. Barnaby knew how to
laugh and enjoy himself. I'm not enjoying this ceremony
one little bit. He wouldn't have liked it much either. He
would have preferred a swim.' Silence. Lucy stepped into
the car. 'Shall we go for a swim? Do you mind?'

It is Goldilocks' awakening. Her hair is still silky and
curly as she could wish. She's a miracle, a little French
miracle. The telephone on her bedside table is still playing
hard to get. 'Now that's enough, Lucy dear, calm down.
Jack hasn't forgotten you, he's waiting for something
fantastic, a little marvel, all for you.' On either side of the
telephone a photograph of Barnaby and a photograph of
Lammert: Lucy's dead. Lucy's lovers. Her life, in one
impeccably straight line. Shortly after the war Elia had
advised Lucy to apply for a job in Foreign Affairs. 'With
hard work and a little patience, in three years they'll send
you abroad.' First posting: the French Mission in Kenya.
All their visitors were delighted with the little French
secretary, and in particular one assiduous Anglo-Saxon.
'*Bonjour*, Monsieur Balsam.' 'Good-morning, Miss Roussel.' The little game went on for a year. Rather more than a
year. Time enough for Lucy to go to France on leave and
while in Paris to buy herself a green dress, which she would
keep for a special occasion. Till the right moment came
that green dress got tried on month after month, every
evening in front of her bathroom mirror in the bungalow
she shared with the governess to the Ambassador's
children. '*Bonjour*, Monsieur Balsam.' 'Good-morning,
Miss Roussel. This time it's you I've come to see. I'm
having a birthday party, and I wanted to hand you this
invitation in person.' And when Lucy arrived, sheathed in

green from top to toe, she had come straight from that balcony in Carpentras, where she had done her homework and won the right to see the world: now her dreams were within her grasp. Barnaby Balsam kissed her hand. 'You are very beautiful, Lucy. I may call you Lucy, mayn't I?' Then he held out his arm to her. 'And I must say thank you, because I know you have waited and kept the secret and the charm of that dress just for me.' In her personal diary, another of her unfinished novels, Lucienne Roussel will make the following entry: 'This is the most perfect day of my life and I'm sure no-one will ever pay me a more delicate compliment'. A month later the former secretary of the French Ambassador will be inviting His Excellency to dinner. A good marriage, 'but she deserves it'. The green dress plays its part again, most effectively. An ordinary little story on the whole, the sort of romantic titbit Lucy loves, not too salty, but tasty, with a slight tang to it, just right. 'We won't have any children, but that's not important: you are my daughter and I am your son. We'll start life together, like children. It's time for recreation, let's go out and play.' Barnaby must have had a balcony in his life too. But Barnaby does not give himself away. Lucy will find out very little about him. She will only be admitted to the day-to-day joys they share together. A magazine story for *His and Hers, Intimate Secrets* or *True Confessions*, revised and adapted by the trolls of the tropical rain-forests, the imps of Guadalajara, the gods of Chandernagor and the witches of Aden. The distinguished career of a lovely but sterile woman: the one bitter note in a full if self-centred life. 'Beyond the Blue Horizon . . .' Lucy is crooning to herself. It is Goldilocks' awakening: no phone call from Jack. With Lammert at Antibes she had gone for a swim. The murderous sea was seeking forgiveness for Barnaby's death. The futile death of a fruitless love-affair. 'Barnaby wasn't the man to blame me for that swim. Our life together was neither here nor there.' 'I beg your pardon ?' 'The French, you know, Lammert, stopped begging each other's pardon a very long time ago.'

Green signifies death. The green of her dress. The green of the Veronese Suite. The green of Central Park in the rain. Grey sky: Lucy's top-coats thrown over New York City. Lucy is lying full length on that beach of thick green carpet. Lammert stretches out beside her. Then moves closer. He takes her hand. Barnaby watches them and smiles. He is proud of Lucy: Lucy is still attractive. She gratifies the master by seducing the disciple. 'That's what I tell myself anyhow, but I don't think I'm wrong.' Lucy calls softly to Lammert. Then she smiles. She calls softly to Barnaby for help. This time she laughs. She is talking to herself. She lives by herself. Central Park's carpet unrolls in front of her eyes away to the north, but without taking off: the rain keeps it earthbound. Expectation keeps Lucy riveted to her apartment. She has almost turned mineral, an emerald in an emerald field, an encrusted gem. 'Lammert . . . Lammert!' Once upon a time in Lusaka a young man and a car were found welded together into one carbonised lump, a black diamond, a clenched fist of bereavement. 'B.O.A.C. Flight No. 713 from London . . . a call for Mrs. Lucy Balsam. Would you please contact the B.O.A.C. desk.'

Twelve noon. It is raining. The day will have to be killed off somehow.

Chapter Five

Rasky is waiting for Luc. On the second day. The nurse
said it was raining outside. 'It's turned cooler. The wind
rose during the night. The sky's overcast. Season of mists',
she had said in a rather precious and affected way, while
preparing an injection. Rasky dislikes the posh nurses one
finds in posh hospitals. The anti-chambers of death can do
without refinement. 'Season of mists' indeed, why did she
dig that up? It's too elegant. Too premeditated. Then there
are all her tasteless enquiries about the sort of night I've
spent. The dreams that enliven my sleep. She tries to peer
into every alcove, into every darkened doorway, prying into
my ancillary amours. Ancillary, yes, she actually said
ancillary. Does she even know what it means? Rasky is
watching her: is it the same nurse as yesterday, or the day
before that? Rasky gets them all mixed up, these white
dolls, well-starched and well made-up, with their bland
remote voices. Could he be slipping away already? Could
he already have cast off some of his moorings, rounded the
first headland? 'Don't move, I'm going to give you an
intra.' The nurse is bending over him. 'Your veins are so
delicate, so temperamental. You must have been a temperamental child, no?' Silence. Rasky thought to himself,
I have always been a child. Then he closed his eyes, deciding that henceforth he would have male nurses only to look
after him. Handsome nurses with hazel eyes, immigrants
if possible, Greek or Sicilian, who would speak Ameri-
canese in their own inimitable way, strongly rolling their
RRRR's. 'Does it hurt?' 'No, I was thinking of something
else.' 'That's the way, think of something else. As soon as
your veins hear me coming, they pop under your skin and

41

vanish. I don't know. Perhaps you've no plumbing system, no blood, nothing inside, you're so peculiar.' Dry little laugh. Rasky bites his lips. He'll ask the doctor to find him male nurses in future. 'I can't stand nurses who chatter, doctor. Besides, I don't like women.' No, he won't say that. He'll simply ask for male nurses in place of the girls. Why else should he be paying? He has no need to account for his actions. He has no more accounts to render.

White is a morbid colour, and morbidity is a pure invention of those who refuse to look life in the face and face up to death, that transferred image of life. All his life Rasky has been in a precarious position, with too much of a good thing, too much money, too much wit, too much charm, and too many full boxes of matches to set light to, just for the hell of it. Rasky left Paris because of his fondness for Luc, he felt beaten, flagellated by life. Professor Verniansmann had told him frankly that the red patches behind his knees and in the bend of his elbows were just a prelude to a slow process of decomposition. 'You are going to decompose before you die. I owe it to you to speak in all sincerity. There is nothing more I can do for you. The only thing left now is to find the place where you can be most comfortable. If there's a deterioration, New York is well-equipped. I suggest the Sutton Hospital. I'll write to them today. And send your case history along.' 'And Luc?' 'His last tests were negative. Still negative. Believe me, that's the truth. And it doesn't surprise me. Some individuals are extremely resistant, one might almost say immune, though no such safeguard could be said to exist medically speaking. I have your friend's case history here. Twelve years of negative results.' 'And Luc?' 'I'm sorry, I . . . ?' 'What am I to say to Luc?' Professor Verniansmann clasped Rasky's hands in his. 'My responsibility ends here.'

White is a morbid colour. Rasky dreamed he was a *millefeuille,* a gigantic wedding cake skilfully constructed out of sticky piles of hundred-dollar bills well-soaked in honey by some God-forsaken pastry-cook, a gâteau oozing fresh cream, a soft paste made of paper dough, no more than a redoubtable and sickly sweetmeat. 'Luc, is that you?' And Luc in all innocence was cutting up the cake. 'But Luc, it's me . . .' What would the nurse have made of that strange dream? A nurse whose pockets are undoubtedly full of scurbius, a nurse who applies her white make-up and creeps out from behind the tiling to play her role in a terminal clinic where a surfeited life runs its course. So Rasky will never have managed to give one thing to the little Parisian high-school boy or to the proud insolent young man—not even the worst of all evils. 'Not even my evil disease'. Rasky's voice resounds through his enamelled room, that immaculate hall of opaque mirrors. A world without shadows.

'Doctor, nurse keeps insects in her pockets, she does, I promise you, I've seen them . . .' 'Don't get so worked up, give me your hand.' 'You don't believe me . . .' 'Why yes, I believe you.' 'You're smiling.' 'Only a little. Close your eyes.'

Anatomy of decomposition: my legs are swelling, my stomach is swelling, there's no feeling left in my feet. Have they chopped them off? Oh, if only I had the strength to tear away these sheets, and heave up this cathedral of blankets! They ask if I want any music: I don't want any music. They ask if I want to watch television: I don't want to watch other people any more, living, talking, laughing, shouting, and going on about what's going on in the world. Colour television? No, I don't want any colour. I want to hide behind the whiteness of my last marble hall. The insects are back again, at home: Luc told me. They are taking over. Taking over from me. I must tell Luc to keep an eye on them. But if I do, he'll get to like them. Start collecting them. Pop them into boxes. Feed them. Study their reproductive system. I know Luc! Quick, I must write to him. 'Doctor, I want to write a letter. Send me someone I can dictate it to, someone who won't understand a word I'm saying. Impossible, doctor? Oh well . . . '. In some places my skin looks so thin it must be almost transparent. I've turned into a fishbowl. Can't eat any more, have to be fed. A baby. Have I still got teeth? 'Doctor, a mirror! Tell the barber not to forget his mirror. When he's finished shaving me, I want to look at my face. I want to know if I'm still able to bite. And scratch. Tell the manicurist to come, I want the feel of the file scraping over my nails and the orange-stick slipping under them, I want them cleaned up, to see my old hands back again. The hands I used to have, when I could still sign a cheque and fondle my favourites, the sailors in Hamburg. Do you know Hamburg? I went there on my own when I felt like sulking with Luc. On impulse. To keep my hand in. Doctor, why are you going so soon? I've got a lot more to tell you!' No music, no television: I'd like a line-up of beautiful boys. Or else a male nurse, just one, who would refuse me everything, but who'd come near me now and again and brush against me. I promise you he'd cure me. This bed is a cemetery for jellyfish. Who was here before me, who will follow me, who, who, tell me that? Show me the list of guests. Tell me what happened to them. Perhaps I can be embalmed, sewn together, patched up, mummified, restored and ensconced in one of those establishments for which New York City is renowned, one of those Beauty Parlors which the capital of the world has created out of its Funeral Homes? Bravo! Fetch me the Manager of this Tomb of the Final Rendezvous, I want to have a word with him. Is it true that he rents corpses by the half-hour or the hour to Ladies and Gentlemen who go in for things like that? Is it true that a dead man's sexual organ is so elastic that you can blow it up with air and, if you get my meaning, sit on top of it? Now don't forget, I see the world as it is. So don't pretend to get all uptight about this business of

44

worshipping corpses. After all, it's a new form of love. And I have dozens and dozens of friends who would leap at the chance to play around with me when I'm dead and pay a fortune for it. You don't believe me? You're the manager, sound out your best clients. It's all or nothing. They like them either too young or too old. And I'm too old. Delightful. I'm bursting. Like an old burst tyre. And if you leave a few open sores, they'll even be able to see what goes on inside while Dame Syphy is dozing in her exotic boudoir. He was beautiful, my Viennese gigolo. He had a curious flower in his mouth and that's what I liked about him, that flower of skin, which brought danger to his lips as they plastered me with kisses. And seven years later when I learned the truth, I felt sure that it was he, a present from him. A flower from Vienna.

And I dreamed last night—or was it the night before, I'm confused, it's like these nurses, I get them all mixed up—I dreamed that I was the whole world and that in me the whole world was cracking up. Phut! And at last I dared to tell it what it had never, as I thought, dared to tell me. *I* wasn't writing any more: my eyes and my words were writing. Romantic turns of phrase expressing love's labours lost were spelled out in the sky, on the skyscrapers (how do the birds manage to get up so high and fly above the skyscrapers, and what do they make of us way up there?) Everywhere I was writing, on every wall and even every heart. Messages like 'I'm going Rasky', 'I am you and you are me for better and better, make of it what you will. Rasky.' 'The scurbius will not win, there will never be a crack in the tiling of my skin. They won't find a way in. That's a promise. Rasky.' Have you seen my name, doctor, all over the walls? Tell me. My name, rising up to heaven, vertically, in erection? Which floor are we on? What's the number of my room, you forgot to tell me. . . .

45

Chapter Six

Second day visit. Five o'clock. 'I was talking to myself, I
even believe I was shouting. The doctor came back. He
promised me a male nurse. Then he gave me an injection
to make me sleep.' 'A male nurse?' 'Aha! Not jealous, are
you?' 'If that's what you want.' 'That *is* what I want.'
Luc folded his arms, lowered his eyes and stared at his
rain-sodden shoes. 'Your feet are wet. Take your shoes
and socks off, sit down over there and put your feet up on
the bed, here, near my left hand. Look! I'm beckoning you
with my finger, like a dirty old man, an aging sex maniac
waiting at the gates of childhood to tempt you out of your
playground.' 'Don't get so excited. It's not good for you,
Rasky.' Luc pushed his chair against the bed, removed his
shoes and put his bare feet up on the white sheets. Rasky
caressed them. 'You are my continent, and this is one small
corner of you I never got to know very well. Still a few
things about you I haven't discovered, you see. You were
always telling me how curious you were, about things like
the flat heels your President's wife used to wear. For you
they symbolized your country, a housebound republic,
self-satisfied, cautious about everything, short-sighted and
God knows what else. Aren't you pleased to discover how
curious your friend Rasky is? I'd never have enough time
this evening, taking one toe after the other, to explore the
whole of your foot. There! Now I'm tickling you, don't
move! Don't say a word! Keep still. It's so good like
this.'

'There was no-one in the Baths on First Avenue. Or such
a small choice of faggots that all I did was watch and
listen to them talking opera and vacations. Rivals for the

47

best sun-tan. I'd bought a package of peppermints as I came in. Lifesavers. Beside the pool, I conscientiously sucked my way through them and then I left.' Silence. 'Those baths are brand new in fact, but do you know they're already full of . . . what do you call them ?' 'Scurbius.' 'So then I went on to the European Baths. I was sure I'd find some copy there for Rasky. They're bigger, older and dirtier. And the boys look much prettier in the dim light. It conceals and flatters them.' 'What did you do?' 'I bought another package of Lifesavers. This one was liquorice. But I didn't have time to finish them. I met Larry. He's twenty. Larry from Allen City, near Philadelphia. He'd suddenly decided to go and spend the night there, because he just gave up his job as gardener. A specialist in lawns. Laying them out, and then the upkeep and the clipping, is that what you say for lawns . . . ?' 'Go on.' 'And I think he told me he'd become quite well-known for his skill in planting and making the desert bloom. So I smiled and asked him where else he planted his seed. He smiled. And he told me he knew right away I couldn't be American, as there was nothing he could read in my eyes or in my face. In other words he couldn't read French. And it wasn't till then that he asked me for my first name. Without a moment's hesitation I told him: Rasky.' 'Thanks.' 'That's not all: the partition walls of our cubicle were metal. Every now and then when we changed positions, we'd knock them with an elbow or a knee, and it resounded. Funny sort of clang it made. We were on the top floor of the building and we had no neighbours. The ceiling was a kind of chicken wire and above it a little red light was shining, very dimly, yet Larry seemed dazzled by it: he had his eyes shut while he fondled me. I mentioned it to him. And he said, as a sort of excuse, that he still had a lot to learn. His love-making was meticulous, captivating. He's young, and I thought that's how I must have been with you, when I was his age. He cuddled up close to me and rested his head on my chest like a child. He had a sharp-pointed chin. For a split second I had the idea that his chin might be a dagger that would plunge into my heart. Later I suggested we went down to the night club in the basement for coffee. A French singer was running through the programme she's going to give this evening. Arabella Blum, heard of her? I told Larry she wasn't at all well-known in France, though I may have seen her name occasionally on posters outside Paris. I even pinned her down as one of those who 'all her life remains a budding star and who never had the luck to have some awful car crash and get out of it alive, *France-Dimanche* and all that sort of stuff.' Larry smiled but he hadn't understood. He can't read French. Then I caught sight of a notice over the bar: *Occupancy of more than 900 persons strictly illegal.* Nine hundred! Can you imagine nine hundred? Then while Larry was kissing my hands, he told me he liked my name, Rasky, and he wouldn't forget it'. 'Thanks.'

Luc slipped his two feet under Rasky's left hand. The blankets over Rasky's legs pulled tight with the weight of Luc's bare feet. 'Look,' murmured Rasky, 'that cathedral over my stomach is pulling a face. She doesn't like you being here. But it's true, you are running a risk, letting me stroke your feet. I could just give them a little tug and drag you away with me. If only I had the strength. But the effort might pull my fingers out. And maybe you don't want to come with me anyway?' 'But Rasky . . .' 'That wasn't a proper question. Go on. Tell me what went on in that basement. You're my personal T.V. set, with just my favourite programmes. Those *Late-Nite Programs* I've already seen before, but who cares, they're always worth seeing again. Go on.'

'Arabella Blum has a big fat bum. A lolloping lump of a girl with long blonde hair not just bleached but like straw. They tried out a few lighting effects: she smiled and she was beautiful. Then she looked over at the boys in the band: the smile had gone and she was all creased, like that cathedral of yours, a real old witch. And then you know what it's like, the Night Club in the European Baths, the Catacombs: all brightly coloured fountains and plastic trees, the fluorescent pool, the mini-Mexican-saloon the Queens Bar, glossy black walls and low ceilings, glossy pink, in beams of light cast from brackets in the shape of a navel or the genitals. Not many clients. They casually cross from side to side in front of the rostrum, pendulous prick swinging below the towel they've tied round their waists. Arabella makes a few attempts to vocalize, bawling out "Up in the sky, ever so high . . ." while she aims one finger at the ceiling. Then for "In heaven above, two people in love . . ." she hugs herself to plump out her breasts beneath her jumper. This evening she'll be wearing a clinging black gown, and she'll look as if she's just crawled out of the wall. She must be making herself up now. 'And Larry?' 'Gone back to Philadelphia.' 'Go on.'

'Lying in a hammock, not far from Arabella, I inspected our export to America. I wondered if I could write a caustic article about her and how my Editor would take it. They say the Bordeaux and Burgundy they serve in New York restaurants is just Algerian wine or wine from Portugal that's had a rough passage. A touch of sea-sickness on the way. But then I thought Arabella wasn't worth a dust-up. She was doing a job of work in a fairies' night club, that's all. And fairies need their little queens. There are worse ways of getting launched. Besides, I'm only another fairy, aren't I?' Rasky smiled. The door to the room opened. A new male nurse arrived and introduced himself. 'My name is Carlos.' He rolls his RRR's. 'Carlos, this is my friend, Luc.' Carlos shook Luc's hand. Luc gave Rasky a sly wink. 'Good grip, you're in luck.' Silence. 'Go out for a minute, will you?' Rasky murmured. 'It's time for my anti-bedsore gymnastics and I'd rather you didn't witness that. There's a different Rasky beneath these sheets, you

50

know. Not a pretty sight. Very messy.' Luc made for the
door. 'But you won't leave, will you?' Luc shrugged his
shoulders. 'Show me some more pictures, won't you?'
No seats in the corridors. Not one window. White
intestines gleaming in neon lights. Another world. Death's
jewel-box. With his hands thrust into the deep pockets
of his blue-jeans, and his head sunk in his shoulders, Luc
shivered. Reality is sometimes so much stranger than
fiction that there's nothing romantic in it at all. What does
romantic mean anyway, in a world that has turned its
back on adventures in the sun and cavalcading crusaders,
a world that has changed hands again and again, been
discarded and salvaged till it has worn quite threadbare?
Luc can recognise himself there all right, looking on the
black side of everything, but a desperate case only in the
eyes of those who refuse to see what stares them in the face
and won't take what is there for the taking: when there's
a crack in the tiles and the mouldering damp crumbles the
cement in the joints, one sometimes wants to peep behind
the scenes. Luc gave a few kicks at the skirting-board, then
he started to count as he paced up and down, his eyes
rivetted on his bare feet. Bare feet at Sutton Hospital: a
nurse came along and stared at him in disbelief. Luc went
on counting, a hundred and twelve, a hundred and
thirteen . . . that's two minutes gone already. A year ago,
just before Rasky left Paris to take refuge in New York,
he had said to Luc: 'Everything that happens to me is
beyond description: my life reads like the invention of
some gay compulsive liar. Every time I tell a story I've
experienced myself, a bit picturesque perhaps but a true
one, bitter or sweet, they never believe me. No-one believes me but you. And I guess that's one of the things that
unites us. Ignites us.' Luc had been careful not to explain
just then how Professor Verniansmann had warned him
that Rasky's disease had taken hold and would follow its
secret course till it finally erupted through his skin, and

51

how Luc had thought of it as a kind of gigolo's revenge. The idea of revenge is hewn from the hard rock of life, and Luc's mind was cut out for such thoughts. Only today Rasky had said: 'I enjoy myself now better at night than I do during the daytime. I love what little sleep I still get. When I'm asleep, I'm no longer a man of property. I myself have been appropriated. Taken over. Determined by another self deep down inside me. And your presence is more real to me now than my present existence, which startles me and bores me: I can't look at anything now with my eyes wide open. My eyes are tired. At night I open our album of farewells and as I rush to meet you, you run take me in your arms. Come closer to me.' Silence. 'You see, I've got tears in my eyes. Strange piece of literature, our story. But I know you don't hold it against me. I'm going to write officially and tell you that I'd rather not see you for a while, for a year, and that it's . . .' '. . . the finest proof of our affection/for each other.' Rasky smiled. Luc burst out laughing. 'Are you finishing my sentences now?' 'When *you* talk, I get the feeling I'm listening to myself. And vice versa.' 'Well, you tell me about my nights then . . .' Luc took a deep breath: 'At night you find out at last what binds us together. You give me everything and I take nothing. All I give you is my No, my refusal. And you refuse to accept it. That's what binds us together. What divides us and unites us, and protects us from the jealousies of others. You tell me to take this apartment. I say no. Anyone else would have said yes. That would be the end. Your company is all I need.' 'That *is* what I would have said . . .' 'At night I start training for death. At night I sleep all alone, with my hands folded over my stomach, laid out like an effigy, and I learn how to detach myself from a life that once I was given and now no longer want. At night, each of us alone in our own little bed, we are apprentices to death. Our fate lines cross, yet still run parallel. Each night we learn a little more about that other dark night, our last one, or is it the first? It's endless. Our greatest gamble.' 'Exactly.' That word exactly. Luc recalls the precise tone and cutting edge Rasky gave it: exactly. It was the parting shot. So Rasky was really going. Leaving the stage, giving up the star part in the one-man show he put on for his own benefit. Turning his back on the one and only member of the audience: a high-school boy he had never quite managed to buy, who had grown into a shrewd but frustrated reporter of a static society from which he was quite unable to detach himself. Human beings love their open wounds. Does Rasky love his bed-sores? Are they the sum and substance of all those trouser-dropping brief-snatching adventures in all the back-rooms and bushes of all the body-exchanges in the world? Buy your International Gay Guide here: addresses of all bars, cinemas and sauna-baths, with a note on every corner of every street or park where time suddenly snaps into a moment of violent action. Exactly. Just enough time for your mind to flash you a 'forever' as stupid as the stick of chalk you're holding when you don't know what to write on life's blackboard. 'You haven't done your homework: you'll get nought. You don't work as hard as the others: nought.' Luc kicked a bare foot against the skirting-board. He hurt himself. And every time it made a sound like a faintly beating heart. A heart that still knows how to beat from time to time. Giving a jump. Exactly. Carlos is coming out of the room. With his right hand still on the handle of the door he places his left forefinger over his lips. Rasky dropped off during his exercises. He is learning his last lessons. It will soon be the final exam. And Luc has faith in him. He'll pass it with Honours and Commendation. Luc will be back at the same time tomorrow, as usual. It's a habit.

Chapter Seven

'Barnaby and I were happy: we mastered the art of never giving anything away, an art that others mistakenly despise.' Lucy hesitates. She had her pen-holder in her left hand, with the *Sergent-Major* (S–M) nib pointing upwards: the ink will get dry. By the time she has chosen the next sentence to write, oh so carefully, with thick strokes and thin strokes, preciously inscribed in her Exercise Book with the help of a writing implement which reminds her of her primary school in Carpentras, the nib will be bone dry and have to be dipped in the inkwell again. Do it properly. 'Oh, that little Roussel girl, the only non-Jewish member of her class, she comes first in everything, and she writes so well . . .'

Lucy re-reads. 'Barnaby and I were happy: we mastered the art of never giving anything away.' And after dipping her S-M nib in the inkwell (dark green ink, very dark), she adds: 'We never let other people into our lives. Our happiness was immaculate, on the surface. Lammert had understood that too. The handsome second string in my bow of life. Paradoxically, the difference in our ages brought us closer. We shared a secret understanding of something that had gone wrong, that part of my past which I had spent so selfishly, and this shared secret shielded us from any attack from outside. Lammert, my Barnaby Bis. I picked up the expression from him. It amused him, made him laugh.'

Lucy gets down to it. 'In a world in which the one re-volutionary gesture left to us is to become a drop-out, unfit for salvage, it may look like nostalgia to try and salvage our impressions of the past. Literature is the prerogative of those whose life has been a true adventure or at least appears adventurous enough to endow a human being with the stature of a god. In the melting-pot of my childhood, in my conjuror's hat all I can find are folded slips of paper carefully instructing me to write, searing my heart with visions that never quite set me alight. A chair on a balcony when my homework is done. Racialism: a whole class of little Jewish girls envious of my hair, who ask me why my parents don't go and live in another part of town. Odds and ends. Little details. The story of a green dress. A series of little adventures: Carpentras, my first prison, to be followed by other prisons: my cousin Elia's ambitions for me, and my bungalow-prison in Kenya, when the governess to the Ambassador's children admired my breasts and begged me to take a shower with her. More prisons, capital cities—those great big villages, and bedrooms where Barnaby spoke to me in whispers as if we were at risk of being overheard, caught by surprise or undermined by jealousy. And there I was fainting away in his arms: there's a first time for everything. No-one was more surprised than he. Amazed. And so was I. The commonplace story of a typist. Now, wherever I go, that balcony in Carpentras is there in front of me. To-day it overlooks Central Park.'

Lucy re-reads: the word 'revolutionary' makes her smile. But weren't the lessons she had learnt from Barnaby the same ones that Lammert had learnt? The *bourgeois* have always been very good at talking revolution. It was their teddy-bear: 'teddy-bear' was Lammert's expression and it reminded her of the tall young man from Amsterdam. 'Will you come for a swim with me? Lammert! I have a date with you this evening, every evening I have a date with you somewhere between West Eighty and West Ninety Street, at Jack's, you know Jack, don't you? Isn't he your hall-porter?'

Lucy has completed her page. She rips it out. It wasn't

56

at all what she wanted to write. She has said far too much all too soon. And no sooner has she stopped than Lammert appears on the scene, undressing on a beach at Antibes on the day of the funeral, at a time when the bathers are on their way home, single file, pa-ma-and-the-kids, in the setting sun. 'It doesn't matter, we still have enough time.' 'You had your swimsuit on under your dress . . .' 'I thought I might come. All alone. B.B. would have approved.' *Sergent-Major* nibs are ideal for telling secrets. They tattoo their marks on the paper till the very last page of exercise books with all their first pages ripped out. Waste of an exercise book. When you are a lady of mature years, you do not *describe* a young man. You go swimming with him, without asking questions. You follow him. He tells you to come and you come. He asks you not to disturb him when he's at his studies and you keep quiet. Barnaby would have smiled to hear about Lammert and told Lucy not to miss 'her last train.' Lucy acted accordingly. There's no rhyme or reason where time or chance meetings are concerned. Who provokes whom and what? When does one start analysing the situation? Before? Or after?

Thick strokes, thin strokes. 'These September refrains may not be beautiful, but they are true. I'm making a big birthday cake. Lammert died a year ago. I'm taking my time. And time creeps up behind me, crying stop thief. I'm playing with words again. I think this is the right moment. But words play nasty tricks on me when it's raining, when you're bored in New York City, when you don't know what else to do with Barnaby's money, when your fur coat's too big and too grand and makes you look like the doorman of a night club that's gone bust. It's raining. *Maman* has gone to sleep in her chair on the balcony. Even the rain won't wake her. In a while, when she puts me to bed, she'll be singing '*Mon bel ange va dormir . . .*'. In her chair on the balcony, well wrapped up in her shawl, a *maman* is a baby. My baby . . .' Page ripped out.

A Barnaby Story. 'Experimental guests, new neighbours from an experimental block of flats, here come Saul Friedlick, the famous diamond merchant we have never heard of, and Gloria Pimpiante, his mistress. We were doing the honours in our house in Park Lane. "Your home is quite beautiful," says Gloria Pimpiante, "nothing in your rooms at all." Silence. The indignant Turner hanging over the console-table in the entrance hall nearly crashed down and broke the marble top of Prince Murat's chest-of-drawers, acquired by Barnaby's father at a sale in the Château de Saint-Cloud. Then Gloria Pimpiante does it again: "It's such a silly name, but I like it, so I'm sticking to it. Besides, Saul won't marry me. You see? He doesn't say a word." Polite smile from Saul. We showed them round the house, a continuous suite of Victorian rooms, Barnaby's art gallery. Every object was his pride and joy. It was my little Louvre. A 1906 charcoal sketch by Picasso discovered at Christie's by John Giveparty, a carpet by Sonia Delaunay made for an ocean liner, and a collection of Chinese vases which Queen Mary on one of her rounds would have loved to slip in her handbag without so much as a by-your-leave: even a queen can be a kleptomaniac. Now come on, that's enough of that. I'm just an ordinary little French girl who found her way into high society and, whatever else she does, should never say a word about her life: put it in black and white and she gives herself away. But Gloria has remained plain Gloria. "Your home's quite beautiful, because there's nothing in your rooms at all." During dinner: "It's delicious, what's the name of that dead bird?" And after dinner, as she took me by the arm: "I adore your dress, it's so simple! It's amazing what you can do with a remnant." "You ought to ask Barnaby the price." Polite smile from Saul. And so on right through the evening. Barnaby's fixed smile of welcome showed how cross he was. But I was the only one who shared his secret and knew *why* he was so cross. Saying goodbye at the door: "Such a delightful evening! When the work's all finished at our place, we'd love you to come to a barbecue on the terrace." A barbecue? Down there on that terrace? Then with the kissing of hands it was goodnight Saul Friedlick and Gloria Pimpiante, our charming new neighbours! "Really," said Barnaby, "they're no addition, they're a subtraction!' Page re-read. It was far more amusing than that, the real thing. Page ripped out.

Is that you, Lammert? Lucy swings round: the *salon* is empty. Lammert? The bedroom is empty, the bed unmade, just the fur rug like an animal that has been butchered, torn apart, quite a slaughterhouse! Lammert, I'm sure you're hiding in there among my dresses? Lammert! Lucy pinches her fingers in the sliding-doors of the closet: a waft of Diorissimo from her clothes. But Lucy is accustomed to the perfume. As it always attends her she can no longer smell it: that's life. Lammert, where are you? In the kitchen, or in the other bedroom? In the morning-room, the boudoir, on the balcony in that chair? There is no chair on the balcony. Lucy picks up her exercise-book. She rolls all the ripped-out pages into a ball. And although she has promised not to do it she calls up Mister Jack. 'Lammert is with you, isn't he?' 'Lammert? Oh no, Madam, there's no-one for you today. But just wait patiently, I've not forgotten you.'

You see, Lucy reminds herself, Jack hasn't forgotten you.

Chapter Eight

Chapter Eight, eight, the figure of death. Every human being is an exercise-book: one after the other its first pages are ripped out till there's nothing left but the cover. 'This was my life. I'm writing this in memory of my life.' Every human being is an open book which one would like to know inside out, through and through and beyond. If instead of the hard biscuit of experimental literature, dry words drained of feeling, we would rather have a moment of vision, the thrill of strong light, the dawn of a day that surprises at every change in the weather, and seasonable emotions, then the Indian Summer is no longer late in coming: which way is the wind blowing in New York City today?

But how does one give up the ingenuity of parable? Good morning Rasky, good morning Luc, good morning Lucy: one of these days the time will come for you to engage in action together, when the leaves in Central Park are turning yellow, then pink, then blood-red. In chapters that bear the mark of death there must be bloodshed. Blood hurts and offends us, for we are all vulnerable, and the mere word 'aggression' brings a shiver to sensitive and fastidious minds. It is the one irritant in a world that prefers the cover-up and pays for the operation with its lies. How can one give up those funny little anecdotes that one finds in the comic panoply of life and in picture-book romances? The only way to know the true colour of a chameleon is to place one on top of another. There is no other method.

The path that leads from jottings in a diary to the final text (byebye, Barnaby Stories) lies over untrodden ground.

And in a world where adventure can be bought cash down in a tourist agency, there are still some innocents who, with the courage of cowards, launch out on the adventure of writing and attempt to set down fresh impressions. And the moment they take the plunge is always at a time when life is most fulfilling or death is near at hand. That is the way things are, and no mistake.

Luc, thirty-three years old, a played-out journalist; Rasky, forty-seven years old, an overblown playboy; Lucy, forty-nine years old, a typist who has gone adrift: here in one act of forty chapters is an account of their attempt to run away from themselves. And while they kill off the insects that devour them, they all still long to go back to nature and the simple life. They would settle for a garden at Petworth in Sussex or at Vétheuil in Ile-de-France or at Joucas just south of Carpentras. Then they would cease their headlong flight from one prison to the next, where they rub shoulders with life's racketeers, professional con-men with stultified hearts, pontificating trendies, a whole gang of pretentious upstarts with a talent for launching soul-destroying fashions. Who cares if one is not understood, providing one understands oneself? And there is always a little of oneself in other people: lying dormant. Who cares about being alone, providing nature still welcomes you with an enfolding embrace, permeates and transports you? A man about to die is but a child that aches to be abducted. A man about to die is a gardener who has just been given the sack: away he goes, but he carries his garden with him, and never before have its sights and sounds seemed more enchanting. They have the hum of life. Everything has its price. A text can be scored into inspiration if your pen, that hired assassin, remains vigilant and resists the temptation to run wild into waywardness. 'The anguish I feel is indelible and can be daunted only by royal blue ink. Anguish cannot bear to see its image mirrored in the written word.' Who wrote that? Rasky: farewell letter No. 713? Lucy: in the exercise-book she left behind at Antibes? Luc: I'll send you my fourth article from New York, where I'll have plenty of time to collect my thoughts. But I'm warning you here and now that it will be about Funeral Homes. I gather that for some time now . . .

Last days of September: an attempt to engrave impressions in phrases like handfuls of sand. Time passes in one way or other. But now time is flowing at will through the hour-glass of a left hand, the same side as the heart, dreaming of the other more pugnacious hand, which is wedded to fountain pen, ball-point, or sharp pencil, those eleventh fingers which expose one's life in a herbarium of words, sensations and memories. 'Oh, these memories, white handkerchiefs soaked in my tears, with their nice white laundered smell,' as Lucy will say. Another page torn from her heart. It is with her left hand that Lucy writes. 'A memory of mine,' confides Rasky: 'You know it always frustrates me to think that my parents never tried to frustrate my inclination to write left-handed. I still do now. Had you noticed I always stick my tongue out when I'm signing a cheque?' And Luc will note the following: 'Memories are like flat champagne. I don't like champagne. There's not a bubble left in the past.' And then he will look at his left hand and that other recumbent, his ballpoint pen. 'I had need of Rasky. I wanted to be a cut flower. In a vase. Rasky was my water, mysteriously replenished in the cunning ritual of our farewells, numerous stitches to hold our liaison together. But how many of us were there? Rasky and me and our buttress, Dame Syphy, our confidant from the very first day. And who else? That grinning gold-toothed nurse who had fixed a vague appointment at Sutton Something.'

The first day of October: in search of danger. With body stripped bare, responsive to every sensation in nature, and with hearts that flap like the door of a derelict house, we shall go to New York City, to the High Spots in this City of Heights, where the Rich can afford the luxury of playing around with death. We shall go to the High Spots in this City of Heights and risk the pursuit of fresh disclosures. After our impressions of the last days of September comes the testimony, told in confidence, of our jailor, New York City, that other world of towers, that concrete musical-box (Scotto in *Lucia di Lammermoor* follows the score to perfection, Sutherland is stiff as a poker in *Traviata*), New York City, that dagger on which, with open arms, one impales oneself. But the wound heals within seconds. There danger is as meretricious as the melodrama of *Grand-Guignol*. You must have another try, casting yourself again and again at the cold steel of the skyscrapers, if you are to find the real dagger at last, the one that bursts your heart like a bubble once and for all. Then everything is fine. To have the will to die. And hear nothing but the dying strains of the world. And the closer you come, the further away they sound. The more you stoop over your past for a hint of your tomorrows, the faster the giddiness fades. The precipice seems tame. The *danse macabre* of burial grounds and funeral homes (Home Sweet Home) becomes almost comical. The lemonade you drink there tastes more like water than lemon. And you can win a free gift of wine from the New America: a Californian Burgundy called Roma. Whoever would have thought it? The cleanliness of New York City stinks.

Balcony: a mother's hand no longer restrains you by hanging on to the collar of your goody-goody sailor suit. Henceforth you can play truant and bespatter your past as you land with both feet plop in the puddles: the big bad wolf has fled. And suddenly you don't care for the edge of the forest, for the day that comes after the day you are living through now, for the time you kill while you wait. Buzz, the phone's ringing: is that Jack? Even words lose their proud ascendance. You merely exist. To knit yourself

64

into the moment, the surface reflection of things. Colour-less. Pretending to notice nothing, but observing every-thing. Pretending not to understand, but taking it all in. Going back to being that child whose Mama withdraws her restraining hand from the starched collar of a unisex sailor suit: a Portuguese Mama or a Mama from Car-pentras or even the Mama of a high-school boy in short pants. For no-one now reiterates those thoughtful loving words of admonition: 'Don't catch cold', 'Don't be too late home', 'You've no right to criticise your parents', 'It hurts us more than it hurts you'. No-one is your keeper any more. Henceforth you are the Lord of your own Misrule.

The October of life, first day: having the feeling that you have nothing, when you have everything. Saying it again and again. Even turning it into a joke: a party game. Play-ing the critic or the quizzical observer when you should be outgrowing your own curiosity. September: first im-pressions, the murderers return to the ideal scene for crimes of solitude. October: how the murderers spend their time as they wait for their rendezvous. Big Jack has too much work, so it's a question of waiting. Taking one's turn. Showing astonishment and delight that the first is surrounded by so much whiteness, the second by all that green, and that the third had scurbius crawling all over the place. That's what it means for the rich to get the blues. Like sugar in a cup of tea, a trifle too much and the delicate flavour is swamped, leaving an oddly bitter-sweet taste behind.

'I asked Rasky to dinner. A young Frenchman called me back, Luc something or other. Rasky's in Sutton. Hospital. He's very ill. He's got so enormous lately! He must have had a heart attack.' 'Oh . . . Don't tell me he has a heart!'

Go round the world with one's fountain pen till it runs dry and you die of thirst with it. Once you're away from the laboratory of words, they wriggle round inside you.

Quite frightening. Farewell letters, fourth articles for editors, or exercise-books, those breeding-grounds for tiddlers fit only to be tipped into mountain streams. A waste of fish-tanks.

Go round the world and find yourself back in New York City, a prison of straight lines, a hard-on prison, so many coffins each taller than its neighbour. The prize goes to the first one to scrape the sky. And in the gardens of Central Park good neighbour Lucy is feeding the squirrels. Honey-dipped popcorn. They adore it.

Leather cushion: his name is Tom. A deserter. A letter from Bombay warned Luc of his arrival. 'National Service Hospital, September 13. Dear Luc. This is Bill. Remember me? We met at the Baths in the Viccola della Palomba in Rome. You were touring round with some old guy who wasn't too bad for his age. About two years ago. I got back to the States just in time for Vietnam. I've just left there now. I beat it with a buddy called Tom. Tom and his leather cushion, you'll catch on in a minute. Tom's a brute, a real butch Marine. He trained himself to leap at anyone who touched him while he was asleep and beat the living daylights out of him. To wake him up, you have to fling his leather cushion at him. Then he clasps it in his arms, bites and squeezes it to death. But he's awake. That's his only kink. He's a great guy apart from that. You see, I've still got a sense of humour. Tom's kind of jumpy, that's all. But it's a gas. So here we are in Bombay. Deserters. First night we stroll around the red-light district. Full of liquor. Quite a party. We share the same bed at the Hotel Victoria and we went to sleep in our clothes, dead drunk. Late in the morning, I opened my eyes. I'd forgotten we were free, far away from Dai Pen or Sac Phan where we were for two years. I turned around and accidentally jabbed my elbow into Tom, who took me for his leather cushion. I wind up with two cracked ribs, my right arm broken in two places and my face one hell of a mess. Specially the eyes. All clawed. Lucky I was dressed or he'd have swallowed me alive. A real soldier-boy, that guy. Now I'm hospitalized for at least three weeks. The army will be on my tracks by then. As for Tom, he's making for Frankfurt via Paris. He arrives the 21st of September, K.L.M. Flight No. 917. I gave him your address. Can he shack up with you for a day or two? Can you help him? He has a load of good stories about the American Army. Maybe he'll inspire you. If all goes well for me, I'll arrive the first day of October. That's it. Love and kisses. Bill from the Viccolo della Palomba. Greetings to your old'un.' A week later, Tom had landed at Luc's with one bag and his leather cushion. 'Hiya, Luc.' 'Hiya, Tom.' He explained that the Americans have two quite separate armies now. One army of shock troops made up of volunteers: the Marines, who have the right to use heroin. And they are trained to kill. 'I'm a good Marine, I know my job. My alarm clock is something I'm proud of. It's just too bad about Bill, he forgot to use my gadget. That's the way I am. When I'm repatriated and they send me back among the pig-butchers of Kansas City, there'll be fireworks, believe you me.' And then there's the other one, the conscript army: an army of pimply students. They are only allowed to use grass. They trip around chewing gum and making mini-war. When they are back home, they'll be no problem. A few good sex and violence movies on the box will cool them down. The psychiatrists say that's enough to keep them happy. Give them an odd murder or two and they'll soon get adjusted. 'Hey,' said Tom, 'catch my cushion. I guess I'll sleep on the floor, O.K. by you?' Silence. 'You're not scared, are you?'

The editor refused the article on the two U.S. armies. 'Everyone knows about that already! You're flogging a dead horse!' Luc shrugged his shoulders. 'Just about all there is left to do in this country.' Smile. 'Now listen, Luc, we're not going through all that again, I like you for what you are and for what we've made of you.' Silence. 'Take a vacation.' The same evening Rasky's telegram arrived. Luc left the keys of his apartment with Tom. 'But who's going to wake me up?' 'Sleep, *mon vieux*, sleep on till Bill wakes you. With that cushion.'

Chapter Eight, eight, the figure of death. At Orly, waiting for the plane for New York, Luc had made a note on a paper napkin: 'The more I smile, the harder it is to forget myself. And the more I smile the more I see myself as the self I don't want to be: intransigent in a country that dreads intransigence and any changes of mind en route, a jester longing to be taken seriously and loved for himself alone, a bumbler aspiring to be a champion nihilist, in short a journalist. My real subject is death. And it's the one I have never dealt with. I have an appointment with death. Rasky's going to introduce me. And if death says one word to me, I shall not be content to answer with a smile. And if Rasky asks me to speak, I shall speak. My smiles unmask me and I hate the sight of myself.'

Later on in the plane, on the same paper napkin: 'I'd like to rip up the clouds, push my arms through the porthole and snatch a piece of that fleecy sky, become the little nursemaid of the gods and creep in beside them while they are taking a shower. The plane is chasing the sun. That's all I can say about this flight. We are catching up with time, that is all, that is everything.'

Chapter Nine

Luc and the trucks. A rendezvous Deep in the Depths of
Downtown. Where the boys are. They leave the office at
five o'clock. Go back home, shower, eat and lie down.
They emerge about midnight, pullovers, blue-jeans and
nothing underneath. Especially no briefs. And Downtown
they go. To the corner of Perry Street and Washington
Avenue. From midnight till three a.m. Get going, Luc, get
going: behind the fifteen-ton refrigerator trucks of those
Chicago butchers you've nothing to fear. Join the rest of
the bunch and let yourself go. There's a police patrol from
time to time, but what the hell. When they reach the place
where 'there's something going on', they swing their car
around and sweep the wasteground with their headlights:
everyone pretends to be scared and makes off. But whatever you do, don't be like those paranoid Parisian queens
who scatter through the shrubs in the Tuileries Gardens
and tear their evening gear each time a driver blows his
horn on the banks of the Seine. Keep cool: and coolly
follow the others. Everyone pretends to slope off, hands in
pockets, looking blasé if a trifle downcast, and then as soon
as the prowl car has gone, everyone is back. The swarm or
rather the swarms reform, the honey flows again and the
sweetness of the night returns, even if it is a cold one; the
City conceals, broods over you, and the bastion of trucks
looms larger.

Off to discover what goes on Deep in the Depths of
Downtown City, in the trucks, behind the trucks, between
the trucks, under the trucks, between the trucks and the
brick walls: the miracle of the magic zipper. And whatever
you do don't forget to wear the right uniform, faded old

jeans, real crummy if possible, with a denim jacket, preferably dark. No obvious distinctive colour. A colour for the night, please. A colour for a man, too. For nancy-boys, phantom-women, do not get invited there. They wouldn't come anyway. For they'd be jostled by sharp elbows into pools of rainwater or smartly bashed over the head with an ashcan lid and sent flying among the crates. Who's this prairie flower? Get to hell, Greta. Go get lost in a Beauty Parlor! Silence. Things like this happen in silence. Searching arms and hands. A couple is formed, soon encircled by a ring of inquisitive men, arms hanging loose, hands ready to grasp their neighbours', eyes peering between a shoulder and the turned-up collar of a jacket, the nape of a neck and cascades of hair, pale faces: the night throws up white gestures of explicit love. One practical observation: you hardly need to stoop to walk under the trucks, which reign over the place like insect kings and queens, giant ants, god-like woodlice. 'This wasteground? It's a parking lot. And the owner has a son who's over there now, see, the little guy in black, on his knees. That's the one. His father knows all about it, it's O.K. by him.' Silence. 'A month back there got to be more and more squad cars on patrol. So Jim, the head man of our Gay Liberation Front, went off to see the Chief of Police. He told him if it didn't happen here, it had gotta be some place else. Told him straight we were only doing what comes naturally, in a lonely part of town. We weren't dangerous, and they'd better be chasing the Puerto Ricans, who mug and murder near a dozen people a night in Manhattan alone. Don't push it, answered the Chief, never more than four or five. O.K., Jim went on, you close us down here and we'll find another place to ring up the curtain. Round Perry Street at night there's no-one but us. Then I guess the Police Chief saw the light. Now he sends his squad cars round just to shake us up. They come and then they go. Long enough to make it all more exciting. Then we pick up

where we left off. Come closer. Look. Some of these studs,
I've seen them around all year. I know nothing about
them, surnames, first names, or where they come from.
But they're here and they're my friends. The only real
friends I have. A load of guys who give and take everything. Then it's goodnight, and not another word. No,
don't talk. Don't say anything. Wow! Is your skin soft!'

A whiff of poppers floating through the air: one puff of
wind and it's forgotten. A young man topples into Luc's
arms. Go on, he's yours. You came for a rendezvous,
didn't you? There are some who stand slightly apart hands
in trouser pockets, with lowered heads. One of them
whistles a tune. It's his way of saying I'm here. The same
tune every night. An old song hit of the thirties: 'I'll walk
behind you on your wedding-day'. Some of them are on
their knees: the skivvies, the working girls. From down
there, looking up, the whole swarm appears like a mini-
Manhattan of skyscrapers resembling one another in the
dark, some taller than the rest, but all upstanding, sure of
themselves, defying the patches of sky in the gaps between
those sleeping monsters the trucks. And inside the trucks
is the beehive. Everyone stumbling and groping. We are all
blind children who have lost their toys, who play with
what they have got. The forbidden fruit. Below the belt, in
front and behind. Toys that are taboo. The smell of brick
and trampled earth. In one corner the chant of an acacia
tree, which has gathered its own small group round it and
beats its branches against the glazed stare of the cabs of the
fifteen-tonners: Indianapolis, New Jersey, Bâton Rouge,
Saratoga, Trans America Highways, a stationary journey
through the night. And the unzipped flies make a V for
victory. Small, large and medium; white, black or chocolate, all tense and tender, a whole battery, a horizontal
forest of mouth-seekers. A little love in a lot of silence, of
grey shadows and night, of anticipation and hard-trodden
earth petrified by feet. Impervious even to water. When it

71

rains, puddles form and last for days. When it has rained too hard, the swarm has its feet in water. Boots. Amphibious insects. A little love: hands that brush a shirt aside, creep up to the nipples, our abortive breasts, and gently squeeze them. Another hand that slides up the whole length of the spine till it lovingly kneads the nape of your neck. And you stoop over the face that has nestled in your gaping trousers. Oddly you feel both dressed and undressed, coveted from every side but possessed for a moment only. And that is what counts. The moment, and after that nothing. Anonymous gestures, wasted ripped-out pages. Nowadays the street-corner is the place for adventure. Between strangers. And when a writer feels that his characters are threatening to turn into himself, he has an urge to cast them out. 'Is your novel autobiographical?' asks a prissy-voiced Prunella. 'My novel is exobiographical: I drive out all those characters inside me who refuse to remain anonymous. All those who speak their name. Luc, for example, my brother or my sister, and *mon frère n'est pas ma soeur*, first lesson in French. My brother is not my sister and my tailor is a rich man. That's not funny? *I'm* not funny. I'm a lugubrious clown. When the writing is sincere, a text is simply a magic trash-can. It's a summary, and it summarizes you. It orientates. It is not a diversion, but a constraint. One has to find out if one wants to exist and see without distortion; come to terms with life and death at one and the same time, since they are sisters, inseparable as Siamese twins, so that when one of them holds out her hand, which is what I ask of her, with the same gesture the other invites me to follow. Luc's editor would say that I am flogging a dead horse. But I have chosen solitude and selfishness and this risk: that I shall see my life as it is and like it for what it is. And go down with it some day or other with a dagger in my back.' 'You're talking like Luc.' 'No, I'm talking *for* Luc.'

Luc caresses the curly hair, a new fleece for his genitals.

Then he lifts his face up and throws his head back: the hands caressing him become more insistent. Throat. Bracing himself on both legs, he can now hear the distant hum of the town, that other place of lights and snack-bars, of Puerto Rican crimes, of Sutton Hospital and Central Park at night, that death-trap: the squirrels have gone to sleep. There's an assassin behind every tree. An assassin with two daggers: one to entice you, the other to murder you with.

Luc is absorbed in the thick hair of the man-child kneeling in front of him. The glutton's knees will be worn to the bone. The swarm gets more and more excited. This time Luc's trousers fall to the ground. What if he lost his wallet or the key to the apartment? The money didn't matter, but Odette's telephone number was different. 'I'm sorry to disturb you so late at night but I've lost my keys. I can't think where. Do you have a spare set?' Luc is amused at himself. Here he is, still behaving like a respectable citizen, in an exorbitant situation. I don't give a damn, he tells himself. Though cold, the stroking up and down his bare legs helps to make him feel warm. Another boy is sucking at his left ear. He is reeling. His senses swim. It's all over. For one second he has seen the city upside down, as if the skyscrapers, like ineffectual darts, had hurtled into the rock and though broken off were stuck there. I am about to die. A wipe with a handkerchief and then goodnight. One last look at the other swarms forming up. Something pulsating, reverberating in that silence, the creak of leather boots as someone kneels, the crack of a joint, someone quietly, very quietly moaning, a plaintive cry so far and yet so near. Tomorrow or the day after Luc will return to play games with the refrigerator trucks, those great coffins for dead animals hanging from meat-hooks. A dictatorship on its last legs. Finality, Deep in the Depths of Downtown. And the Police Chief can sleep in peace: there or elsewhere, in every city in the world, the creepy-crawlies congregate in silence. Between leprous-looking walls they celebrate their rites. And an acacia tree mutters as the cold wind wraps round it: soon winter will be pointing her finger. Luc smiles. Pulls up his trousers, tucks his shirt back in and zips up his jacket. He has not lost his keys, nor his wallet with Odette's phone number. 'Goodnight gentlemen with the flowery lips, sons of Vienna or wherever, I shall have a good shower to wipe away the kisses and caresses of Dame Syphy, lest she too were present at the party. But Professor Verniansmann told me I was immune. *Blindé.* And in the language of New York City that means blind, doesn't it?' Luc could almost feel ashamed to be saying this out loud, all alone and at a distance, from the sidewalk. He wanted a long view of the wasteground to see if he could make out those clusters of shadowy figures. Thirty-three years old, a life of second-rate reporting, and sometimes, when he *did* put his heart in it, an odd comment from the boss in the style of: 'You don't spit it out, you just dribble.' Basta. Luc is talking to himself. Released. He feels a sense of release. There opposite, sandwiched between the trucks, the night secretes its little hoard of gluttony and illusion. He likes that. He'll be back.

Chapter Ten

'How many beers have you drunk? Burp! You're belching, you're not used to it. How many?' Rasky's tomb: Luc carefully gives a double turn to two of the locks on the door of the apartment. Bong, bong, bong: three in the morning. Wan light from the chandelier in the lobby. Just by the Louis XV wall-clock over the marquetry chest-of-drawers seven red roses were wilting in a vase, beside which were the pigskin gloves that 'Monsieur has been wearing recently, because he didn't want anyone to see his hands'. Bong, bong, bong: gravely the clock strikes the hour, twice in succession. In Luc's mind time takes a tumble. What is it now in Paris? Ten in the morning? Bill is waking Tom up, hurling the leather cushion straight at his face, and Tom leaps up like a rabid dog. Luc smiles. Lights: this is the exact replica of the apartment in Paris and the apartment in London. The same Persian rugs (Caucasian Shirvans chiefly), same Louis XVI chairs (which are genuine, which are fake?), the Embarkation for Cytherea, Leda and the Swan, Young Man Nude, Nature Morte with Pheasants, reminders of the *Grand Siècle*, ponderous gilded frames and spider-like light-fittings indirectly and subtly suffusing these masterpieces of the past inherited from a Rumanian father and a Portuguese mother. Luc has not unpacked his suitcase. All he will do is open it. And now and then, like a magician, slip one hand inside to pull out a clean shirt or a pullover the colour of night. Not even a pair of briefs. He doesn't need them anymore. Nude in a pair of trousers: New York and its trucks.

Luc is taking a shower. Alarmed by the splashing of the

75

water, the scurbius run for safety behind the tiling. Two or three of them perish, drowned. 'Pity. They're so nice, they don't hurt anyone.' But what do they all get up to together behind the tiles? What if Luc could penetrate their world? Luc shuts his eyes: the water stinks of chlorine. Greenery-yallery, boiling hot one moment, ice-cold the next. Luc shuts his eyes. And now he's blind, very tiny, behind the earthenware tiles, sniffing the flat odour of the walls and the fat odour of cement, and all around him a seething mass of scurbius, wriggling and jostling together, sometimes devouring one another. On the other hand that waterfall, the shower, that huge Niagara signals danger, death by drowning. 'Who are you?' 'I'm the new boy.' 'Show your belly. Show your wings. Turn around, what are you, male or female? You're in a mess, you're scratched all over. You're a softy, a phoney. I can see nothing, but I know you're good for nothing. Get out of here.' Luc opens his eyes. Smile. End of trip to the land of the scurbius. Shiver. He turns off the shower, dries himself and in his bare skin explores his friend's tomb on tiptoe—a place he has never really wished to share in London, Paris or anywhere else. Anywhere else is here. The parquet creaks. A forsaken smell has settled into the furniture, the cushions and the armchairs, not excluding the lampshades sitting on top of the Chinese vases which are stationed, always in pairs like sentinels, on either side of the desk, the fireplace and the sofas. And here's the air-conditioner that has broken down. Luc leans forward to examine it. He hears a sound like clinking, but infinitely faint, like the click of something mechanical, blurred and far away. With both hands he picks up one of the lamps and directs the light through the grill on the machine. The lampshade falls off, a blaze of light: choked with scurbius, bunches of them, coiled like entrails, a black necklace of death untidily stuffed into the metal box. The lamp slips from his hand and smashes to pieces. Luc feels hypnotized, fascinated by the insects. He slides his fingers over the grill, claws at it with his nails, wrenches it off, plunges both hands into the seething black mass now terrified by the sudden light, and hurls the scurbius, whole handfuls of them, into the library and over the sofas. He cries out. Shouts for joy. Then he sucks his fingers: he's been bitten, but no, scurbius don't bite. As he grabs them up he crushes them in his hands, which turn black and blue, ink-stained and sticky, bruise purple. Grateful for its deliverance, the machine is soon functioning again. The insects fall to the floor in clusters and seek refuge under the rugs. Luc tramples all over them. 'I'm the new boy and I'm killing you.' Rugs encrusted with the murdered assassins. Soon Luc's feet are as black as his hands, the ink blots the patterned rugs, splotches the parquet. My God, tomorrow, Odette! 'What *have* you been doing, Monsieur Luc? Whatever has happened?' 'Don't come in, Odette, don't come in.' 'Monsieur will never know.' The scurbius scurry off towards the bedroom, en route for the bathroom. Luc blocks the path with books: The World of Late Antiquity, The Oxford Book of French Prose, Seurat—An Analysis of *La Baignade à Asnières*. Now Luc is rocking with laughter. The scurbius launch an attack on his legs. They slide off. 'You stupid buggers, I'm made of marble.' He slaughters them with his hairbrush, with his comb. He *will* stamp out this teeming murderous scourge. He has stumbled on the underworld: the other world. He knows his own strength, being so much bigger and more powerful! Pursuing one scurbius after the other, he returns to the library, a huge necropolis of books and pictures, and one by one he crushes every beast, shifting the furniture to track down every fugitive. The perfect little killer. And the wall-clock strikes the hours, the quarters and the halves. Time passes, with the slow clip-clop of an old man with a wooden leg, very very slowly. Rasky is housing a murderer. A black murderer with wings incapable of flight, wings

77

quite unable to beat you off, wings that have grown accustomed to the ins and outs of the body, to something infinitely small, a scourge that goes to ground, musters its strength and makes its presence felt at the very last moment, when all is lost. When everything cracks and splits and leads you off to Sutton Place, where you enter the hospital. That is all. A one-way ticket. With a phone call, later, to Mister Jack to ask him to employ his well-known talents as seamstress and make-up artist. Meanwhile Luc will have cleaned up the apartment. Or rather fouled it up. 'But I did it for your sake, Rasky.' Luc is stifling, he opens the window. On 72nd Street the yellow taxis are making one hell of a row, an endless procession of taxis. Other insects, other colours, another kind of death: there's a metre, so you have to pay. The apartment had looked greyly forsaken. Now it was inky black. Graffiti scrawled everywhere, on floor, furniture and walls. A burial ground for the scurbius. Luc goes to sleep on the sofa, in the shadow cast by Rasky, the shadow of their last night. He whimpers. And now he shivers. He wants to die. Burp, too much to drink.

Chapter Eleven

'I have something for you, Madam, but you won't be alone.' Three in the morning. Mister Jack's voice is extremely sharp. He's a businessman is Mister Jack. If you like to push it, a promoter of one of the most recent branches of Show Business. 'I'll come at once', murmurs Lucy. 'I repeat: you will not be alone'. 'But I've no choice, have I?' 'Obviously not.' 'The address please, Mister Jack, so I don't get it wrong, like last time.' 'Freemary's Funeral Chapel, 230 West 74th Street.' '230 West 74th Street, thank you, Mister Jack.'

Kenneth's smile is part of the ritual, the ceremony. Lucy Balsam stays put in her apartment for a day or two, then suddenly she comes out, divinely fresh, smiling and relaxed, slap in the middle of the night, calling for a cab, joking with the hotel bell-boy about yesterday's weather and fore-casting tomorrow's in a style indubitably British. That dame's a *real* lady. Odd, these nocturnal rendezvous in New York City. Kenneth examines Lucy: grey tailor-made, black scarf, curly golden hair. No hat. 'Here's your cab, Madam.' 'Thank you, Kenneth.' 'Thank you, Madam.' Ten dollars.

There are two Lucies that Lucy knows very well and has firmly under control. Lap-dog Lucy, the spoilt poodle, superbly groomed, the one other people see. Gentle docile Lucy, killing time in luxury hotel suites: and the only sweet thing about them is their name. Bitter suites. And then there's that other Lucy, a client of Mister Jack's, the nocturnal communicant, the Lucy that rips out the pages of her exercise books not to speak of the pages of her life, the Lucy who burrows into the back seat of a taxi intent on having a closer look at death. The Lucy who talks to herself, quietly, very quietly, so that no-one shall overhear her. The Lucy of the beach at Antibes, with her first glimpse of a naked body. Her first young man. Barnaby grins in his grave: after the teacher, the pupil takes over the tender-hearted minx. Good for her. The taxi plays its part in the ritual too: Lucy is taking stock. She doesn't like drinking: she has never been a drinker. She doesn't like gambling: she has never been a gambler. She is alone: and she has never been alone. And in those darkened bedrooms (Barnaby hated the light) she has experienced and shared the poignant feeling that time is standing still and that getting to know someone else endlessly sharpens one's curiosity. The echo of a whisper, the wonder of a desire that nothing can impair. Every evening there came the shared secret of the green dress, a courteous thought and gesture perpetuated by constant repetition. Beholden to no-one, Barnaby and Lucy were like blinkered sleep-walkers, creating all around them the darkness that drew them together. Such were the thoughts running through Lucy's mind as she stroked one black-gloved hand against the other, each finger smoothing the pigskin down till the gloves were like marble. Everything could have started again, with Lammert. Everything. Lammert was sincere.

Shortly after the accident at Lusaka, Lucy Balsam got in touch with a company in London. She wanted to have Lammert's body brought home. 'But there are no remains, Mrs. Balsam.' She was given Mister Jack's address. 'He'll know what can be done, they're used to this in New York. We're not.' Mister Jack, when consulted, admitted that relations with Zambia were very bad indeed. 'I can't help you at all, Madam!' Silence. 'Besides, your friend has been cremated already. Pardon me if I sound tactless, but there's very little we could have done. I'm grateful my colleague in London gave you my address, but . . .' How can one explain what followed? Lucy began to worship the bodies of the dead. And Mister Jack was able to offer this as an alternative. Why? Why not? 'I have a date with you, Lammert.' Lucy taps a fingertip on the glass partition between her and the taxi-driver. 'Here, here . . .'

Columbus Avenue. Deserted sidewalks. Not mentioning the actual address is also part of the ritual. Kenneth is burning to find out. And Lucy doesn't trust him. The cab disappears round the corner of 72nd Street. Lucy is alone at last. Mister Jack has not forgotten her. She loves the paving-stones of the sidewalks, two steps for each one, left foot, right foot, then on to the next. Standing tall on her high-heeled shoes, Lucy feels she can measure up to New York City, a nice little giantess in four-league court shoes: she has a date at last.

There goes the envelope containing the money. Hatchet-faced Mister Jack, in his light-brown suit and his squeaky white shoes, with a flower in his buttonhole and his smarmy hair plastered down, shows her the way. Scented corridors (cut carnations, the flowers of death) and soft music (a rumba on the Radio City organ), and then it's the chapel. 'Here you are, Madam, now you know where you are.' 'Thank you, Jack, thank you.'

Lucy takes a deep breath and clasps her hands together as if about to pray. The leather-lined door closes behind her. Empty stalls, and way ahead in front of her a platform bathed in pink light that turns to yellow, then green and finally blue, before going back to pink again: the scene is set. This evening, a young man laid out on a bed. A nude young man, and round his head a crown of tiny pillows embroidered with 'To Bobby forever', 'Silence is stupid', 'We forget you not', 'The sooner the better'. Enlivened by silken cushions, rainbow-coloured petit point, ribbons and fol-de-rols, the young man is receiving his unknown friends for the last time. Round him are standing about thirty men, upright, rigid, motionless and silent. Lucy remains slightly apart. She pulls off her black scarf, which is choking her,

81

and unbuttons the jacket of her severe tailor-made. She feels relaxed and happy. Observation: a skilful use of cosmetics almost conceal a rosy little necklace round he throat of the corpse. Bobby has been strangled with a shoelace. So Lucy starts flirting with Bobby's story. Imagining. Drawing the main outlines of her imaginary tale, deciding on the chapters and the acts, writing a novel, the story of a life, that other life, the life of that young man. Quickly. Very quickly. There is no time to lose. A ventilator starts up, overlaying the silence with the continuous purr of a motor blowing out air, perfumed this time with incense. The lighting settles at blue. The ceremony begins. One of the men approaches and caresses Bobby's face, trailing the tip of one finger with infinite delicacy round first his eyes and then his mouth, lightly brushing the chin, and then tracing a path to the sculpted lacquered hair. Using both hands, the man alters the position of some of the dark curls that tumble over Bobby's brow. Then he smiles and beckons the others to approach. Hands are stretched out. Soon Lucy can see no more. They are all bending over him like surgeons, but in leather jerkins, in black or dark-blue overcoats. It all looks rather like a film in slow motion, the fleshing of the hounds, or an attempt to analyse an action shot of an Olympic champion clearing the cross-bar at seven metres. Pole-vaulting. And at the highest point the image is frozen. Heads bent, faces down. The cloth of the overcoats quivers. The leather of the jerkins creaks and the light imperceptibly lowers. Something flickers out, oblivion descends. Not a word. Not a sigh. Lucy is watching the group, a dark flower folding in on itself, falling into a trance. Lusaka: the whole world is saluting Lammert, caressing him. Lammert's body is back. Lucy is proud to think the whole world is paying him homage. Jealous of those other caresses, she will wait until the others drift off, one by one, before she greets her friend for the last time. Her friend as he was, dashing, all of a piece, that fine day in Antibes or those other fine days in Amsterdam, when Lucy pretended to sleep in the morning while Lammert typed away at his desk on the final pages of his post-graduate thesis on the Relationship of Central Government to Regional Organisation. Full stop. Organ stop. Period. 'O.K., I'm jealous, but I'm a good sport.' Lucy smiles at the thoughts going through her mind. She removes her gloves and slides the black serpents into her handbag, folds her hands, then shuts her eyes and opens them again: Lammert is here, all in one piece, not burnt to cinders. And without the car, that glove-box of death. In her own language '*la mort*': more frightening than death, with an extra-strongly rolled 'R'. A word that growls like a bad-tempered dog, confident it can still scare you in a world that has almost forgotten fear. Crazy, isn't it? Lucy bites her lip and she can just taste the blood in her mouth. She is quietly sobbing: isn't that why she came? It's all working out. She drops her handbag and makes her way towards Bobby, pushing the men aside. But what are they doing? 'Let me through.' 'Sssshhh.' Poor Bobby is bespattered, his legs pulled apart, his enormous penis blown up like a fire-balloon ready to burst. The men are vying for the privilege of straddling Bobby. 'Stop it!' 'Sssshhh!' The blue light has dimmed, the smell of incense is asphyxiating. That rumba can be heard again on the Radio City organ: Mister Jack in his office must be replaying the tape. One tape is enough. 'My clients always overstay their welcome, anyway.'

One by one, with lowered head, the men creep quietly away, a strange smile playing round their lips. They thought they had run the whole gamut, but there was still one pleasure left: to stretch out one's fingers and touch death, face to face, to pleasure oneself in death. In ceremonial silence. Bye-bye, Bobby. Soon Lucy is left on her own, except for one tall man, bald, with a vacant blue stare, his hands in the pockets of a still unbuttoned topcoat. So it is in his presence that Lucy wipes the body down with her black scarf. Cleaning Bobby up. Putting the child-man straight. She crosses his hands over the hairless belly, peerless navel. She closes the compass legs, presses out all the air from the pumped-up member, lays it coyly to rest and brushes it with her lips. Then she wipes his mouth and eyes and tidies his curly locks. The black scarf is soon soiled. Motionless, the man watches her, staring into space. His gaze is the same as Bobby's. Death costs money, death means cash. The Maffia had already laid hands on the Funeral Chapels, now it is involved in the Last Farewell trade too. 'And don't those faggots love it, above all when they've passed their prime. They come to give the K.O. to the youth they've left behind. That's my guess anyway. It's no business of mine. Little envelopes, that's all I'm after.' Word of Jack Verazzi. Neon lights. The incense-blower stops its unpleasant continuous hum. The slightly stooping figure of the man in the buttoned topcoat pads quietly away. Mister Jack opens the leather-lined door. 'It's all over, Madam.' He walks up to Lucy. 'I promise you'll be on your own next time. But it's not easy, you know, I have many requests.' 'I know, Jack, I know . . .'

Chapter Twelve

'Carlos washed me and I went to sleep. He has the hands of a god. I live again.' Silence. 'Sit down and talk to me.' This time Luc sat on the edge of the bed. He took Rasky's left hand between his two hands and squeezed it. 'You're hurting me, what's wrong?' Silence. Rasky is rotting away, everything except his eyes. 'Well, say something.' 'Gold Wig committed suicide in Paris the day before yesterday. It was in the papers here this morning, a paragraph on the first page. You know one of his plays is on Broadway this season. What publicity! His angel must be pleased.' 'And how did he do it?' 'He jumped from the window of his hotel bedroom and impaled himself on the railings. You know the story about the sailor.' 'What story?' 'Well, I heard it from you. You remember: three years ago Gold Wig picked up a sailor. He took him up to his hotel room. The sailor demanded money. Started beating him up. In the struggle Gold Wig lost his wig. And this was the way you told it: feeling stark naked, Mademoiselle de Paris had the sort of brainwave that could only come to a naked fairy.' 'Stop it.' 'So Gold Wig told the sailor that she did have some money in travellers cheques, but she hid them in a little plastic bag hanging on the left-hand shutter outside the window.' 'Stop it, this story makes me laugh.' 'Gold Wig opened the window and told the sailor to look. As he leant out Gold Wig pushed him and out he went to get impaled a few floors down. Four storeys were ample. Legitimate self-defence. No case. Missing: one sailor.' 'Luc, there's no point going on.' 'Three years later the hotel management must have given him the same room. And Gold Wig mistook himself for a sailor, so out he went! Goodbye!' 'Haven't you any other stories?' 'But that's the sort you like.' 'No, I don't.' 'There you are, that means you do.' 'Luc, you know me far too well.' 'May I kiss you?' Luc leans over Rasky and Rasky shuts his eyes. 'Now when I kiss you, you close your eyes. Teacher has forgotten the lessons his pupil has learnt by heart.' 'By heart?' Luc places one kiss on Rasky's lips. 'You smell nice.' 'Carlos looks after me properly.' Silence. 'I *would* be amused if you were jealous of Carlos.'

'And it was Gold Wig, wasn't it, who lent his apartment in Rome to a hard-up gigolo and told him to feed the geese he kept on the terrace so as to make his own *foie gras*. A snazzy idea for a snazzy lady. You remember that, Rasky, or you're kidding! After three months in the States he got back to find the gigolo glowing with health and the geese as skinny as those French Academicians who live on manna from Heaven. No mystery there. Instead of using the money to stuff the geese, the gigolo had stuffed himself.' 'Stop it, Luc, stop it!' 'And you know the excuse the gigolo gave. He said he'd fed them every day—with vaseline on toast.' 'Luc, these stories don't amuse me any more.' 'O.K.'

'Right, would you like to hear about the trucks last night?' 'No.' 'After the trucks I went for a beer at the Cellar, a new bar for Gaymates. Notices everywhere: You'll never be that man your mother was.' 'Stop it.' 'Or in the toilet, the Girls' Room, there was this one: Microphones, tape-recorders, movie-cameras and other listening devices absolutely forbidden.' 'You don't mean it?' 'You see, it does amuse you.' 'Not very much. Careful. I can feel your weight. It's as if the sheets were peeling my skin off. Sit in the armchair, the way you did yesterday, barefoot. Will you?'

'When I got back to your place, I broke a lamp. The one on the desk in the library, next to the air-conditioner. It slipped out of my hands, just like that.' 'Just like that?'

86

'Yes, I thought . . .' 'Thought what?' 'I don't know. That there were scurbius in the machine.' 'Are you sure?' 'Yesterday I was sure.' 'Why yesterday?' 'This morning there was nothing. I'd had a few drinks, you know. Odette came in to clear up. She asked me why I'd been sleeping on the sofa. She asked me to give you a kiss for her too. I've done that already.' 'And then what?' 'I rented a bicycle and went for a ride in Central Park. I followed a beautiful boy on a black bicycle. We raced each other round. Then we lost each other. Then I found him again. I asked him if he felt like drinking some American champagne. He wondered what that was. I told him Coke. So we took our bottles with us and went to lie on the grass in a secluded spot. Not far away our bicycles were propping each other up, making love.' 'And you two?' 'Oh, nothing like that. He told me the story of his life. I don't think he was interested in men. And that's exactly what *did* interest him. He wanted to talk about it. Does that sound complicated?' 'Commonplace. Go on.' 'Well, I quoted him some lines which you taught me one day in the Bois de Boulogne: I think at times that I should like to be the saddle of a bike.' 'And he laughed?' 'He laughed.' Carlos came in. 'You know,' Rasky murmured, 'I think I shall get some sleep today too. Till tomorrow, dear Luc. Thanks for your stories: they get me out of my shell. I read that in Sevy Erravan's diary, a comment on one of his writings. Something like: today it's an effort, this text is my nut-cracker . . .'

Chapter Thirteen

'And today,' murmured Carlos, 'I'm going to give you a facial. The doctor gave me the O.K. Close your eyes and let yourself go.' A creak from the pulleys. Rasky can feel the bed hoisting him up, his body being folded in two. 'I hope it's not risky? I'm afraid of slipping.' 'Take it easy. Let yourself go. I'm used to this. Twelve years I've been in this hospital.' A smile from Rasky. 'So you started when you were twelve.' 'Almost. At first I worked in the basement, in the laundry, with the Chinese. I was there for four years. They began to show an interest in me. I didn't want to change, but something told me there was a future for me here. The hospital paid for my evening classes. I got to be an orderly, then a probationer, then a fully-fledged nurse. But that wasn't good enough for me: I came to specialise in skin-care. I wanted a job on this floor. It's very well paid and its fascinating.' 'Which floor is this?' 'Pardon me?' 'Which floor . . .'

Rasky has closed his eyes. But the image of Carlos offering his services with a little glint in his eye, a glimmer of affection, is engraved on his retina. A profile, an outline. Carlos has rolled up the sleeves of his white uniform, revealing his bare forearms, a forest of hair that Rasky carries in his mind. A foretaste of the night. 'That's right, keep your eyes shut.' And Carlos' hands are laid on Rasky's face. His fingers. Ten fingers (he counts them) and the palms of the hands pressing on his cheeks, sliding to the nape of his neck, and then back up to the ears to get lost in his hair. 'Your hair's very silky, you have very beautiful hair.' And Rasky thought to himself: 'I'm still in luck, he might have said *still*.' Rasky smiled. 'So it makes you smile when I pay you a compliment,' Rasky screwed up his lips and tried to say no. 'What does that face mean?' 'It means no, no.' 'Don't move.' Carlos steps away from the bed. The sound of flasks and of absorbent cotton being pulled from a box; and in the area of space contained in that white room there was another presence, a second visitor beside himself. 'It's odd,' thought Rasky, 'Luc doesn't give me that impression any more. Luc is part of myself, he's inside me, either I know him too well or I don't know him at all. Luc always held back. Never gave out any feeling of presence.' The sound of footsteps: Carlos approaches again. 'And now here's Carlos lifting me up. I feel as if I'm upright, almost on my feet again . . .' 'What are you thinking about?' Silence. Carlos smoothes his ointments over Rasky's face, greasy ointments, wadding, cooling creams, wadding, tonic lotions, wadding, massage. 'Is that good?' Carlos lays two pads over Rasky's closed eyes. 'There now, keep quite still. I'll be back in ten minutes.'

Suddenly Rasky can see the hidden nature of his disease: there is nothing of him left, not one patch of skin, not one ounce of flesh which he is master of and can call his own. He has been taken over. A flabby lump. Each one of his cells has collapsed. The firework display is over. The only thing left is his eyes, agate eyes, glass marbles. And what if he were going blind? Suppose it wasn't wadding over his eyes, but the tear-soaked handkerchiefs of Dame Syphy, the queen who ruled over his life? Perhaps it was she who had paid for Carlos' evening classes. Evening classes, night classes. 'Carlos!' Sometimes ten minutes can last a long time. Time began to weigh heavy, turned violent again. 'Carlos!' Rasky can hardly feel his right arm, and his left arm not at all, all stiff and numb with pain. 'Pins and needles!' Rasky has even lost the strength to tear off the pads that blind him. He has taken flight into Carlos' jungle of hair, and as he runs he collides with a low-hanging branch, he is blinded with blood and cries out for his mother; and far away he can hear his mother singing her *fado*, that heartfelt song which repeats one single word again and again, a word that means everything, something like Saodad, I am alone with nothing to cling to and nothing to hold me. Totally adrift. Saodad. 'Carlos!' Rasky is calling his mother. 'Carlos!' The door of the room opens. 'Now then, what's all this . . .' Rasky makes a feeble attempt to move his fingers, 'You want me to hold your hand? You sure are just like a kid!' 'Take the pads off, Carlos.' 'Just three minutes more. You can trust me. With me, you have to get used to following the treatment right through to the end.' 'But I'm blind, I'll never see anything again.' 'Come on then, come on . . .' And Carlos gives a friendly laugh. A tiny laugh like the echo of a laugh. 'Here goes.' He removes the pads. 'Don't open your eyes just yet. Careful now. That's the way.' Hot towel, cold towel. He walks away from the bed, then comes back. 'Open your eyes.' Rasky can see himself in the mirror Carlos is holding out to him. He no longer hears what Carlos is saying. He is looking at himself: is that him, if not who else, is that the face which Luc had kissed, are those the lips that Luc had brushed with his, is that the object Carlos treats with such courtesy? This is the mask of Dame Syphy, a blurred forgotten face, its features merging into a shapeless ball of flesh, this is the face of Rasky. 'Is that me?' 'Pardon me?' Rasky looks at the happy smiling Carlos. 'You are pleased, yes?' 'Very pleased, Carlos.' A movement of the pulleys and Rasky is back in the horizontal position. 'Thanks, Carlos, thank you.' Rasky wishes he had the strength to bite his lips: he has seen himself. Rasky closes his eyes. Carlos slips the sheets from under his body, changes the disposable wadding, slides out the bedpan and fusses round the bed. 'Your friend was waiting in the corridor. He asked me if you'd gone to sleep. I told him you had.' Silence. Carlos has stopped moving. Carlos clears his throat. He is removing his jacket. Rasky opens his eyes. Stripped to the waist, Carlos picks him up very gently, with one arm under his armpits and the other under his knees, and gingerly sits him down in the armchair. 'There we are. The doctor said I could do this too.' It was the discovery of another New World, the odour of Carlos' skin and the hair on his chest like all the forests of the earth. 'I'll make you up a brand new bed. You'd like that, wouldn't you?' Rasky feels like a sack of old clothes, a bundle of dirty washing. He leans his head on his left shoulder. 'There's nothing wrong with you, you know, nothing at all. You've no strength left, that's all, and we're going to make you strong again. You won't be the first person we've got back on his feet. You do believe that, don't you?' Rasky smiled. Carlos rips off the mattress-cover and bundles up the soiled linen. Then he flicks the fresh cover and the clean sheets out with a snap. 'You'll see, you'll pull out of it. A month or two and it'll soon be over.' Carlos takes hold of Rasky again, more energetically this time, sweeps him up and away, so that Rasky seems to be flying high over the forests. 'And now you're going to go to sleep. And sleep soundly, I'm sure.' Carlos puts the skeleton cathedral back over his legs. Then drapes the sheet and blankets over it and tucks them in, giving a final tap to the pillows. Carlos lays his left forefinger over Rasky's lips. 'Not another sound now. Good night. Pleasant dreams.'

Chapter Fourteen

There is one corner of town where the sidewalks are break
ing up because they have been forgotten. Luc is crossing
the city from East to West, and then from North to South
along 11th Avenue. He never even knew there was an 11th
Avenue. A forlorn Avenue. Zooming taxis slow down as
they sight him. 'Hey man, this ain't no place to walk
around all alone.' Luc doesn't care. He waves his thanks
and pursues his own little course. He likes these pitted
sidewalks, the wastegrounds fenced in with gaping chicken-
wire, the brick wedding-cakes—monuments to Il Popolo,
La Prensa, the Direct Syracuse Company, and the electric
signs spreading their leprosy over the ox-blood walls. In
this part of town it is no good trying to adjust one's footsteps to the paving-stones. All that is left is a series of
puddles and holes, chunks of broken cement and jagged
cliff-like curbs, as if the Avenue was waiting to bite at the
lone pedestrian. There in West Side New York, the town
disintegrates and empties. Even the warehouses are dead,
stifled with dust, their eyes barred by decrepit Venetian
blinds, half-open fans sending out desperate signals in grey
and black as they pick up the rare winking lights in the
street. Forlorn advertisements.

So Luc, clenching his fists deep in the pockets of his
jeans, his eyes fixed on his feet and the unpredictable sidewalk, starts meditating on his futile journey. But the whole
of life is a futile journey. All you can do is to fake the
mirrors a bit, touch up the reflections of places and people
and set them out like pawns at those spots which best
flatter your vanity or your sense of unreality. 55th Street:
plumes of steam are emerging from vent-holes in the

middle of the Avenue, and the wind shapes them into cork-
screws, or is it they that shape the wind? Who is responsible for what? Luc smiles. Shrugs his shoulders. He
goes. And if he had failed to make a success of his life, he
would make a success of his death. The corollary was
important. Had he been able in some piece of writing to
develop this paradox, reveal its mechanism and describe
its fleeting strengths and weaknesses, he could have
gambled on the throw of the dice and risked winning all or
nothing: the emotional impact of a text is not something
one can control. 49th Street: empty rusty garbage cans.
Luc walks round them. Puts the boot in. And laughing says
to himself 'that's the sound of my life, I'm riddled with
rust.' And that text, which would have taken account of
his very last moments, Luc would have taken pains to
ruffle it up. That's the style, tousled literature, something
different, unlike anything else, owing nothing to anybody.
And he would have sent that text to his editor, who would
have slipped it in a drawer. 'No topical relevance.' 42nd
Street: death. At last Luc comes across someone. An old
fellow dragging his feet, who belches and asks Luc some
incomprehensible question and then aims at his feet a
gobbet of astonishingly white spittle. The end. Injections.
That other anti-chamber of the lady with the gold-toothed
good-bye grin. 'Hey man, hold it, I got somep'n to tell
you.' Luc crosses the Avenue when the pedestrian light is
red. He gets grazed by a taxicab madly honking as it
hurtles past. A cry in the night. Then another cab. Luc
dives for the sidewalk opposite, the west side, and goes on
walking Downtown, to the Downtown trucks and the boys.
He feels hungry, so he stops off at a coffee-shop. No-one
else at the counter. The bartender drags himself to his feet
and holds out the menu. The bartender squints, each eye
splaying out sideways. Luc feels he no longer exists. This
guy is looking elsewhere. Menu: From the Grill. Hamburger 100% pure beef...75. Cheeseburger...85. Our

94

Speciality: California Burger (with melted cheese, 2 strips of bacon, fried onions, lettuce and tomato)...1.30. Hamburger DeLuxe (with french fries and salad)...1.35. Cheeseburger DeLuxe (with french fries and salad)...1.45. Luc chooses something DeLuxe. For the L in DeLuxe. He wants to see how that capital letter tastes. The bartender goes in for remote control, lobbing the hamburger on to the grill so that it lands with a flop like a dishcloth. Then he picks up an enormous dill pickle in his fingers, slaps it down on an oval plate, flings on three lettuce leaves and smears the hamburger with cheese. Another ritual. It is late. For quite a time Luc had waited in the corridor for Carlos to emerge from Rasky's room. But Carlos must have taken a different route to avoid him, or slipped out during a moment's inattention. Luc was dazzled by the strip-lighting in those tunnels, uncertain of the purport of his whole trip and the real urgency of his presence, but quite certain of the nature of his encounter: he had some *other* rendezvous in this dagger-city. A nurse had jolted him out of the torpor in which his thoughts had plunged him. 'The hospital's closed to visitors. You can come back tomorrow at five o'clock.' It was then that Luc had decided to go Down to the Depths of Downtown New York, on foot; it would take quite a while, but then he would arrive just in time for the ceremonial highlights. DeLuxe, a half-cremated Cheeseburger, caramelised. Luc smiles. The man behind the counter is looking smug. Luc downs it, than he's off again. 33rd Street: a plane is crossing the sky, winking its navigation lights, as it makes westward to San Francisco, Tokyo, Bangkok, Teheran, Athens, Paris, completing the circle: imbecile! 39th Street: boys sitting on the sidewalk. Sniggering. Luc pretends not to hear. With a flick of his finger one of them aims his cigarette to land just in front of Luc. Luc crushes it out with his foot. Laughter behind him. He quickens his step. Then he tells himself off, he's not scared. He walks at a normal pace. Deep in the left pocket of his jeans he clasps the keys to his apartment. In the black night of his pocket every key becomes a metal scurbius, a chilling emblem. 25th Street: '. . . and if I *had* produced that text, it would have used up what stamina I have left, the last shreds of integrity which still guide me through a world that favours and rewards all those things which destroy objective vision, plain dealing and the sort of frankness that puts on the gloves and packs a punch called scandal. But life is a scandal, and so is the death which life brings in its train. Gloves are boneless hands, but they simulate the truth. Had I had the time to write that text, would I have put on those gloves? That's enough, Luc, have fun and keep going.' 17th Street: a fine confusion of sidewalks and buildings. Little doll's houses, spruce and intimate, are still sticking it out between the old watch-dog warehouses. Soon it will be the village. The village in the town, on the fringe of everything, a plaything. 13th Street: and if Carlos has any luck, Rasky will give him everything and Carlos will take it all, for he belongs to the race that takes all, strong-armed and cute-arsed. Maybe for him Rasky is the chance of a lifetime. A backstairs road to riches. Rasky's wallet is an open sore too, the first of Dame Syphy's lips to part. Luc will not even offer him his jealousy. Piece by piece Luc has stripped down the mechanical systems that govern his own society, its administration, his own little world and the World at large, and everywhere the working parts were at odds, the just ordering of their rhythmical functions set at nought; all one could do was lie low and wait, or else go roaming through street after street till you reached those Downtown wastelands, where a good-looking man will undo the buttons of his shirt and offer you a whiff of his torso, a damp and weary kiss and a bout of vigorous legerdemain. 10th Street: Luc turns into Hudson Avenue, then right into Bank Street and left into Washington Street. There lies the wasteground with its acacia tree and its Trans-

96

American trucks, aluminium arrows packed tight in a parking lot; and behind the trucks with one stride Luc steps into oblivion. He feels great. He takes the geography and the vastness of the City with him. Invigorated by his walk and happy in his quest, he deserves the moment to come. It is crawling with men. He falls on his knees for his first brisk and brutal contact and he feels as if his ears will soon be wrenched off.

He also feels as if his jeans are going to split. Hands are busy undoing his shirt. A button snaps. 'If you have any mending, I'll do it,' Odette had said. The honk of a vehicle in Washington Street. Police? Everyone stands and buttons up. False alarm. They start again, but the cards have been delightfully shuffled. Hell was invented by nostalgia. Hell is something very simple. You don't go down to it. Hell is on the level: without realising, you walk straight into it. You have to be alone, that's all. And have no-one to write to, to whom you can say 'You are my mentor: thanks to you, words like courage and hope still have some significance. Thanks to you, I am still on my feet, a battling character.' Nice work if you can get it. The world snores away on its pillow of lost causes. An encounter: he is tall, Italian, and offers himself with a swagger, motioning the others to accept his invitation, to go up and fondle him. And if the other man's organ fails to please him, he drops his hand: disgrace! Another man takes the other man's place. Kneeling in front of him, Luc gratifies him, raising his eyes to admire the adolescent's torso, towering up like those other skyscrapers in that other City. And now for the first time Luc feels giddy.

Chapter Fifteen

Ladies' afternoon: Lucy has decided to celebrate Bobby's last farewell in style. She is lunching alone in the snack-room of the Plaza. Alone at last with Barnaby and Lammert. Barnaby on her left, Lammert on her right, and opposite her an empty chair. 'That,' she says to herself, 'is the chair reserved for what my future holds in store. The other ladies are hat-collectors. They inter all their memories in a hat, one stuffed bird, three lace flowers or an aigrette. That is not enough for me. I am the sort of lady who needs to offer her hand to someone, a lady ill-disposed to be a fading photograph.' Lucy is buttering pieces of toast, which she intends to leave behind on the plate, but she butters them all the same and spreads them with caviar: her children's lunch. A child is a dead person who challenges and haunts you. An image of perfection that one destroys. A new inmate in the prison of life. Till the day when life opens the prison gates, between two yachts or on the road to an airport. So, unless they seek refuge in hats and tea-party chit-chat, ladies turn nursemaid to their memories. Yesterday Lucy had wiped Bobby's body clean: death must be clean. A fine excuse to come into close contact and catch the chillness of death.

Lucy observes the elegant world of the living in their hats and ties, carefully mouthing their words, eagerly devouring the titbits she would leave behind on plates embellished with the coat of arms of some prince of the hotel trade. Another kind of nobility. Lucy observes this world in motion, charming and rich, or ostensibly rich. A world that Barnaby used to black-list. One must not invite Tom, Dick or Harry any more. One must stop seeing the

So-and-So's. And refuse all invitations from Mr. Upstart or Madame Parvenue. Lucy got rather annoyed. 'What about me? Who do you think I am?' 'You are Lucienne de Carpentras, a new version of Gabrielle d'Estrées.' 'You're joking.' 'No, I'm not. Typists make the most beautiful queens in the world.' All Lucy and Barnaby's friends had appeared on one black-list or other till they had all been amiably interred. 'I want no phoney friends or honest hypocrites, no fake socialites or genuine decadents to find a place in our life. I want nothing false to come between us two. So I don't want anybody. Since I've known you, the only thing I welcome is the look of curious enquiry from my students when at times I manage to interest them in my course. To be able to go on teaching is a luxury to me, for these young men endow me with a treasure that the world has lost: curiosity.' Lunch at the Plaza: Lucy lays her hand on the armchair to her left. She is stroking Barnaby's hand. Then she leans forward and with a similar gesture strokes the armchair on her right, smiling at Lammert. 'If I could tell you what I did last night . . .' And she smiles. And is silent.

A matinée at the Saint Paul's Theatre. 'It's a very good show, Madam,' Kenneth had said, 'and it's a very good seat. Oh, thank you, Madam. Thank you.' A five dollar tip. Coaches loaded with ladies disgorge their cargo: ladies in white, yellow, black, red, green, nothing but ladies, parties of ladies, Guilds and Congresses, and Societies for Lonely Ladies. Lucy is reminded of the outlying districts in Carpentras, where no two houses are alike: today it is no two dresses alike, a telescoping of colours and fabrics and styles of cut, special offer patterns from stateside super-markets, a crazy explosion of diverging fashions, a fusion of anything goes, an amalgam of tweeds and satins, of evening slacks for the afternoon, of hostess gowns in sunset hues, of tunics with pompoms and Mexican embroidery. Every language is being spoken in sharp, shrill tones that pierce the eardrums. The doors are besieged as though a throng of startled birds were jostling their way out of one cage into another, for a different show. Lucy feels she sticks out like a sore thumb, in her plain black tailored suit and her black scarf. Hatless too. Just that blond helmet of unruly curls, which still recall those Saturday dance-nights at Vaison-la-Romaine and those first boogie-woogies with Michel, the solicitor's son from Séguret, the little village beneath the peaks of Montmirail. Montmirail: and wasn't it in New York, in an obscure room of the Frick Collection, that she had renewed her acquaintance with the mountains of her childhood in a picture from the School of Provence? 'Your ticket, Madam.' Lucy opens her handbag. What has she done with her ticket? She gets elbowed out of the way and her feet get trampled on. 'I'm not used to this sort of thing', thinks Lucy. She finds her ticket tucked into her pigskin glove.

The name of the show is 'Pepper'. With song and dance: a musical. On stage they're doing a job. No mad delirium, no sparkle: it's a Wednesday matinée. Three thousand ladies are however spellbound. They have come to Broadway. Some of them reserved their seats months ago. Now they are proudly settled in the orchestra stalls. They aren't bored by the boredom of it. They have found what they came for. Noise. It takes their minds off things.

So Lucy reminds herself that she is killing time because time has not killed her. She thinks about the ripped-out pages of her exercise-books, those accursed notebooks. And the blessed daily dose of irrevocable fatigue. She thinks how she would have smiled in the days of cousin Elia if she had been told how listless she would be when she was fifty: grey on a green field. If she had been told what passion would obsess her in her fifties: black scarf on a white body. How she would have laughed if she had been told the story of the lady and the corpses. The mother of the

101

night. When you have no children, you create dark
shadows of your own. And when a sportsman brings
cartridges back with him from the shoot, next Sunday is
the focus of his thoughts. What could be more natural?
Barnaby disappeared too soon. And Lammert disappeared
too soon. And Lucy still knows how to kill, kill time. She
still has a body and the money you need to come to a
quick decision. Matinée at the Saint Paul's Theatre:
Barnaby is on her left, Lammert on her right. They are
dressed up as Brooklyn ladies and pretend not to recog-
nize Lucy, but they are there all the same. And Lucy is
trying to like a show that she *dis*likes. All this screaming
and bawling, that rhythm. Nothing. It all means nothing.
And by the time the first half is drawing to a close and an
entire new set has emerged from the back of the stage, a
shoddy structure of scaffolding and steps crowded with a
chorus of dancers and singers chanting 'Pepper! Pepper!',
Lucy has gone back to the day before, to the moment when
she and Mister Jack were about to part company. 'Wait a
moment.' Mister Jack is mounting the podium, scattering
the cushions round Bobby's body. 'They'll come in useful
again,' says he in an overloud voice. And then he laughs.
'This ain't the last Bobby we'll see in here.' Then he steps
down into the hall of the chapel, kicking the embroidered
pillows to one side. 'Now we're all set.' And he rubs his
hands, this professional dancing partner, this Maffiarite
dealer in death by stages. 'You're gonna like what you're
gonna see.' He has opened a small panel behind the leather
door and pressed a button: organ music. Then another
button: bright red light. A third button: and behind the
podium, a heavy metal door swings open on a blazing
inferno, a kind of huge oven into which the podium disappears, as if swallowed by fire. The door closes again.
Lucy gets ready to go. 'No, it's not over yet.' Mister Jack
is standing up straight behind Lucy's back, his hands
clamped on his client's shoulders, forcing her to remain

seated. 'You'll see, the best is still to come.' 'But I don't want to see.' 'You've paid for it, haven't you?' Lucy closes her eyes. 'Another twenty seconds. One, two, three, four, five . . .' Lucy had counted the seconds too, when she was going through the customs at Lusaka. 'Urgent message for Mrs. Lucy Balsam.' The message had read: 'Sorry, I shall be a few minutes late. On my way, Lammert.' 'Twenty-seven, twenty-eight, twenty-nine, thirty. Now look! For God's sake, look!' Mister Jack presses Lucy's head back against his belt and with the thumb and forefinger of both hands makes her open her eyes. Lucy, alarmed, sees the door open, the podium return and instead of the bed, the sheets and the body, just a tiny heap of black cinders. 'Quick, eh? Did you enjoy it?' Lucy lets out a cry. In the Saint Paul's Theatre three thousand ladies are applauding. It is the close of the first half.

During the intermission, Lucy tries to push her way out. But the ladies, all these other women, are blocking the exits. Gossiping, greeting one another, exchanging compliments, admiration, flattery. Between one of the staircases and an attendant selling candy Lucy cowers trembling in a corner. She pulls her black silk scarf very tightly round her neck and presses her arms close against her hips: she feels cold. The intermission bell rings and the ladies go back to their seats, leaving behind them a debris of chocolate boxes, candy wrappings and plastic cartons of orange and grapefruit juice, the straws ringed with traces of lipstick. The lobby has emptied. The orchestra strikes up the overture to the second half of 'Pepper'. Lucy makes her escape. 'Pepper' is a flop. All she can remember is that podium. She wants to be alone again in her green apartment. Mister Jack has promised to call back. Not this evening, but tomorrow or the day after . . . In the snack-room of the Plaza the waiters polished off the caviar sandwiches meant for Barnaby and Lammert.

Chapter Sixteen

Dream. Inside Rasky's body. Rasky is inspecting his body,
the blood of Vienna and the blood of men. His father used
to say, strongly rolling his RRR's: 'Don't take artists as an
example to follow, they're parasites.' Parrrrrrasites! And
this is the voice that follows Rasky round as he makes a
tour of himself, inside himself. The hope of sleep that
Carlos brings can be restorative only if Rasky first restores
himself. That at least is the logic behind his tour of
inspection. Odette follows him round with a sewing kit and
needles. 'You have to do the stitching inside out Monsieur
Rasky, otherwise it will show.' So Rasky is trying to sew
himself together from within his own body. Hips, belly,
the sagging chest and the genitals, all from the inside, so
as to knit together what once endowed him with a
erection. Now he can have a close look at his disease. His
deepest wounds. Figures, he is full of figures and squan-
dered banknotes, and bars choked with fumes and giggles.
With a flower in his buttonhole, Rasky surreptiously
fondles the young kids as he moves around. But only at
belt level. And try as she may to hoist herself up on bus-
kins bejewelled with paste, Dame Syphy can never reach
higher than one's fly. She's a dwarf. Though sometimes,
in the spring perhaps, she manages to leap up and plant a
flower between your lips. Let's get moving.

Tobogganing through his veins, Rasky scrapes away the
pox that gnaws at him, telling it to 'go away', as if with a
cry he could clean out his body's sewers. Odette shouts to
him to wait for her, she knows how to set about it, the
housework that's her affair. But Rasky will not listen. He
has always liked to do everything for himself. And he has

only one night left to refurbish his appearance, the way he looked in the past, with a body like any other man's, innocuous, yet subject to adornment by desire. Then Carlos might take him in his arms and carry him off. And perhaps the journey from bed to chair and back again could last another lifetime. Basta. Kaput.

Not one corner of himself left now, where Rasky does not feel like a stranger. So he climbs up to his eyes. Only the eyes remain intact. He had suspected that. Now he is sure. Right, he'll start with the eyes, all round the inside of his eyes. He'll scour and pumice and drive out the salty fluids that make his skin so puffy, bite into the blisters that refuse to burst, excise the germs and pustules and break up the malignant cells. The only trouble is that these deserted labyrinths remain unknown to him. 'Monsieur Rasky, you're going too fast', cried Odette. Rasky is going round and round his eyes, cleansing, scraping, polishing. 'Monsieur Rasky, it's making me giddy.' It's the big dipper, the roundabout within, the ultimate travelling circus. Quick, quick. Carlos is due at any moment. 'Look, Odette, here and there and there.' 'Thank you, Monsieur.' With the two of them together, perhaps they'll make it. When Carlos comes into the bedroom tomorrow morning, perhaps Rasky will be able to get up and walk towards him, suggest that he calls a taxicab and reserves two tickets by air for Paris. Or anywhere else. Wherever Carlos wants to go. I swear by bare arms and a torso. 'I've done it, Monsieur.' 'Right, Odette, now there, there and there, hurry, there's no time to lose.'

You don't go down into a dream: you walk straight into it. That's on the level too. You don't go down into an evil pit: you walk straight into it. That's on the level too. Ascent and descent are myths, good only for the cheap morality of hypocrites. Life has to be confronted. It's on a level with you. And the reverse side of life, the dark side, the absence, that other void, that's on your level too. 'Good idea, isn't it, Odette, this sewing job?' Now it's the ulcers round the neck and under the armpits. Odette is throwing out whole buckets of blood polluted by the still suppurating sores. 'More thread, Odette, more thread.' And Odette takes from her apron pocket spool after spool of flesh-coloured cotton thread. 'This won't notice, Monsieur, I promise you.' And Rasky sticks a needle into his skin, pulls the thread through and knots it where the tension is greatest. 'Help me.' 'But Monsieur Rasky . . .' 'Help me.' 'I shall hurt you.' 'Go straight down to my stomach.' 'I'm afraid to.' 'Oh, no, Odette, not now.' Rasky starts laughing loudly, very loudly. It resounds all over the house. The landlady is moving out. The dwarf is packing her bags. For good. 'She's going, Odette, she's leaving!' 'Who's leaving, Monsieur Rasky?' 'I'll tell you all about it.' 'Oh, Monsieur Rasky, you must be joking.' In the first light of dawn Rasky will be sewing up the tips of his toes. Left foot. Odette has dropped off to sleep over the final stitches. Right foot finished. 'Odette!' 'It's finished, Monsieur Rasky. How do we get out of here?' And Odette's voice becomes far off, faint, and fades away. 'How *do* we get out of here?' Rasky wonders. He opens his eyes. Carlos is standing by the bed, asking if he has had a good sleep. Rasky tries to hold out his arms. But he can't. Dream dispersed.

Chapter Seventeen

A small boy is playing with Kenneth in the entrance hall to the apartment building. 'Why are you breaking your Dinky cars?' 'So some of them will be smashed up.' The kid smiles. 'I want some smash-ups. So I can play car-crash!' 'Don't you like your Dinky cars?' 'I can't play cars if I can't play car-crash.' 'And you bust up the new ones?' 'You bet I do, watch!' And the boy jumps on a little blue Mustang with both feet. 'New cars get into crashes too, you know. They sure are the craziest. I mean, Pop hasn't paid his off yet, and if it got smashed up, he'd be real wild.' Kenneth gives the boy a playful little pat and goes to meet Lucy. He calls the elevator. 'You didn't enjoy *Pepper*, Madam?' 'Not altogether, Kenneth.' 'Madam's not feeling well?' 'Not too good, Kenneth, but it's nothing.'

Lucy alone in the elevator. The indicator light bouncing rhythmically from side to side like a ping-pong ball suggests that the elevator is doing the same, but the gates finally open on a luxurious carpeted landing muffling every sound and gleaming with Venetian sconces and reproduction Louis XV console-tables arrayed with plastic flowers. Veronese Suite: no matter how long it took, in the end the green would shade first into grey and then black. As soon as she had closed the apartment door behind her, Lucy untied her evening-scarf and removed her jacket and her blouse. The constricting bra, a spurious lover, squeezed and stifled her. She took it off. And with bare breasts, sitting in front of her desk with her legs crossed, she searched for an exercise-book from which she could still rip a few pages. She needed to write. She needed company. She wanted to talk to someone. She wrote.

'I had noted down on a scrap of paper a few magical phrases that were meant to guide me through this adventure with exercise-books. *The balcony at Carpentras, The yachts at Cannes, The airport at Lusaka*, those I remember. But the others, what happened to the rest of those magic spells, buried, resurrected, recorded and then lost? I must have thrown them away with some of the Kleenex I use to remove my make-up. I am alone with my pen, this martyred exercise-book, my adventure with detail, my inventory of the commonplace and these impressions which are not impressions but which impinge on me all the same and then leave their mark like the negative of a photograph. The negative of what I shall never be: a draper's assistant who has sold out of ribbons and is not ashamed to admit it . . .'

Lucy bends over her exercise-book and her S-M nib. In that position her breasts, pressed together, look much prettier. They are eighteen years old again. They need no uplift: they are uplifted by the text. 'My pillow is my foetus. The little girls in the primary school never stop pulling my hair because I am not a Jewess. In that pillow, I live. And the longer time passes, the further I retreat in time. To be tempted by the irrecoverable is my way of being revolutionary. Barnaby would be pleased: I learned his lessons well. All I am is the dying fall of a note on the organ. Impossible. My one vocation is oblivion. And if I try and emulate my Prince of Kenya (green dress) and lash out at the ignominious or the hypocritical, at ambitious flatterers or upstarts, it is because I have no desire to burden myself with other people's baggage. I have no hat-box: I never wear a hat. I have only one box, for my pillow: I travel around with my pillow, childhood and solitude restored. A return ticket, please, just one . . .'

Lucy looks round. There is no-one in the apartment, yet

110

she feels spied upon. Write, to kill the intruder. Lucy writes: 'Dialogue with the intruder. Essay. Come closer and ask me the questions you want to ask.' 'What are you writing, your memoirs?' 'Every word that's written is a memoir. Understand that I am a world within the world. And the other, the big one, the one with the capital W, that one I can only see through the optic of my dreams. Every night I run away from myself. Every day I get arrested by the force of reason or the police for non-payment of accounts. And I get put inside. And so I write. Just like that. Just like this. Look: I am waiting for night to fall. Then it will all begin again. The more I run away, the larger is the prison I return to, unless it is that I am growing smaller and smaller, shrivelling up, as I observe the walls round life, the march and lamentations of mankind. Men in this century have very quickly learned how to stop listening. Their cries are almost inaudible. And then the day comes when one goes deaf oneself. The further I move outside myself, the further in I go. The closer I draw to life, the more insistently death shows herself, sidling up and beckoning me to keep her company. So then I go and pay my respects. While I am writing with my left hand she takes my right hand in hers. Then all by herself she laughs, grips my hand and squeezes my heart, as though she wished it would break a little sooner, before its time was up. I shall never define with sufficient clarity the daring circularity of the process of writing, the urgent drive to turn experience into fiction through the magic and passion of words. The need to checkmate one's own anguish. The image of an insect watching me while I take my bath and make myself beautiful in case Mister Jack should call up. Do you know that the walls of the Veronese Suite are swarming with insects? Though the building is not an old one. I shall have to complain to the owners.' 'So what you're writing is autobiographical?' 'No.' 'You're making it up?' 'I'm living!' 'You no longer

111

think about what you're saying?' 'I only think when I'm writing. I no longer listen to what is being said around me. Except from time to time, just now for example, when Kenneth was playing some game with a little boy in the entrance to the apartment and the boy was stamping on life . . .' 'Here, I'm throwing salt on your exercise-book. It'll bring you luck. One last confession: if I were two blank pages in your exercise-book, would you speak to me? Answer me frankly.' 'I'm only frank in my dreams. Death guides me in the daytime, but at night I thrash her. She deceives me, with everyone. A formidable couple of lesbians we make. I wonder why people always find lesbians formidable? Anyway, in our partnership I'm the butch one and I'm a brute.' 'You haven't answered my question.' 'Every question is a cheat. A question mark is a rifle shot that puts the truth to flight. Neat take-off.' 'You like coining phrases. Do you find them all equally satisfying?' 'No. The lone observer can only incarcerate his thoughts in prisons, if possible of the very latest style. Modern, with all the comforts of the unexpected. The lone observer can only turn back in his tracks. What I write is merely the preface to a preface, and then the preface to the preface to the preface, ad infinitum. So I tear everything up. The deeper I dive, the more profound are the depths. And the deeper the breath I have to take on the surface of my world. Extraordinary. Autobiographical? But I'm not looking for myself, rather I try to lose myself en route. Barnaby tended to make fun of my exercise-books. He used to say: any literary critic who was mother of a family, would turn her nose up at all this and make an obscene comment, such as . . . she doesn't even spit it out, she dribbles.' 'Maybe, but I am sincere. The more I write, the more I rip out. And the more lost I get. Mission accomplished. But you're not listening any more.' 'Correct. Put that down in the obscene pages of your notebooks, on the white paper you defile. I'll leave you this love of yours, as

112

you've failed to find the other sort. Good-bye.' 'Wait, don't go! Listen, I did find the other sort of love. I found it but I lost it . . .' The intruder departs. Exercise-book closed again. Entry recorded. Silence.

Lucy lays down her pen next to the ink-well. She inspects the exercise-book and the interrupted dialogue. This time she will not rip out the pages. She will read them again tomorrow or the day after, while she is waiting for a call from Mister Jack. She will revise them, cross things out and mark comments in the margin in the style of the school-mistress in Carpentras. 'Obscure', 'Imprecise,' 'Elaborate . . .' Lucy smiles. Isn't that a sound rule for life, a cosy formula to mask one's own inertia? Lucy stands up and gazes down on the exercise-book from a great height. She feels so tall she towers over everything. She stretches, lets out a little gasp and smiles. She goes and lies down on her bed, enfolds her pillow in her arms and is soon dreaming that she is stamping on her exercise-books in order to play 'smashed-up books'. And then she'll say to Kenneth: 'I can't play exercise-books, unless they've had a crash. You watch.' And with both feet she'll jump on the day's entry and rip it apart with the pointed toes of her black shoes. And Kenneth will give her a playful little pat on the shoulder. Lucy will go to sleep. Afternoon in New York City: 16.45.

Chapter Eighteen

16.44: the siren of a police car wakes Luc up. A barren night. A dreamless night. He has been robbed of one night. Unless his dream was slow in coming and the siren got in first? Luc can only remember the crazy taxi that brought him home in the morning, very late, dead beat, with sore and tender knees. Before he went to bed he had had breakfast. He had left the lid off the jampot and the scurbius had come and emptied it. 'Whatever you do, don't leave any food about. Put it all away in the ice-box. They'll devour anything.' 'Who's they?' 'The little beasts, you'll see, they get everywhere. When I come round to clean up I'm always scared I'll take some back with me. That's why I turn out my bag before I go. I don't want any of these things in my place.' Silence. 'I do have *some* insects at home, but not these. I don't want any of these'. 'Why not, Odette?' 'Hideous black brutes, they are. Besides, they won't die. I've tried everything, every type of insect-killer, and the harder I try the faster they breed. But not a word to Monsieur Rasky, mind. He mustn't know that since he left there are hundreds and hundreds of them . . .'

Luc threw out the jampot, the wrapping round the butter and the bag the bread was kept in. The empty sugar bowl he put in the sink, together with the teapot, where several scurbius had drowned in their attempt to reach the teabag. Then he went back to the library and sat down at Rasky's desk. 16.52: he is going to be late. He will keep Rasky waiting. Fair enough. He shuts his eyes and concentrates, with his head in his hands: suddenly the night restored his stolen dream. Hurriedly he removed the typewriter cover, inserted a sheet of paper and started typing:

'An imaginary tale. My adventure. Tomorrow or the day after. I am sorry to say that I noticed nothing. I turned up at Kennedy Airport two hours before departure. I was flying back to Paris, worried because I had not written the fourth article I had promised my editor. I had nothing to say, nothing. The cosy scandals of my own country are of no interest to me, and the ups and downs of my private life in New York were strictly private. All I need tell you is that I had spent the previous night at the bedside of one of my friends who died of exhaustion, a weird sort of death. I freshened up in one of the restrooms at the Airport. I had plenty of time: I called the two American friends staying in my apartment in Paris to warn them I was coming home. And shortly before I boarded the plane, I took a sleeping pill. I am extremely susceptible to that form of barbiturate. It was my first trip on a Jumbo jet. I don't like large aircraft. I settled into a corner at the rear with a cushion tucked behind my neck, shoes off and a rug over my feet, with my fastened seat-belt well in evidence, so that none of the air-hostesses would wake me during the flight. I went to sleep at once. I never even realised that we had taken off: I was asleep by then. And that is what saved me. That and the seat-belt, plus the fact that I sleep with my mouth open and my face all screwed up. So I have nothing sensational to report. I saw nothing. Heard nothing. Perhaps you will think it too ironical if I say that the only thing I *can* tell you is the name of the barbiturate in question. But then I should be accused of advertising. So here you have before you a reporter who has passed up a good story. And who does not regret it. Such ironies are part and parcel of my life . . .'

'But it must have been terrible when you woke?'

'Not even that. I was jolted out of my sleep. For one instant I thought the barbiturate was slow in taking effect and that we were only just leaving. Then I noticed that everyone else was asleep. Or looked as if they had fainted.

Oxygen masks were dangling all round me. So then I thought that the plane must have gone through a storm and all the passengers had passed out, except me. All this in a split second. At that precise moment the landing wheels hit the runway. I looked out through the window on my left: I did not recognise Orly. I looked to the right: an air-hostess was lying in the gangway, her jacket torn. And I could see a spot of blood. I closed my eyes and shammed dead.'

'Were you searched before embarkation?'

'Yes. I was even asked to open the case of my alarm-clock. It's shaped like a cube, with no audible tick. It always worries the police. The customs were very strict. And efficient. I believe they even delayed our departure a few minutes.'

'And you just shammed dead, was that all?'

'What would you have done in my place? I had no idea what was going on.'

'Were you scared?'

'I was doped with barbiturate. I went back to my sleeping position. I said to myself, "they'll come and wake you, don't move, you'll find out what's happening soon enough, besides it's only a dream". Then I heard some shots. The plane had just ground to a halt.'

'The pilots were dead?'

'As I found out later.'

'And then what?'

'*I* shammed dead, as I said. No-one else was moving, so I kept still too. I heard a few more shots.'

'The hijackers were dead?'

'As I found out later.'

'And then what?'

'I heard the ambulance sirens. The airport was all lit up with searchlights. I opened one eye, just one. Everyone's doing the same as me, I thought, everyone's shamming dead . . .'

'Then what?'

'The Red Cross removed the seventy-three dead bodies.'

'You counted them?'

'This time I opened both eyes. I was frightened. It was only then that I did feel frightened. A nurse came to me and cried out: "he's alive!" They took me away on a stretcher. But there's nothing wrong with me, you know, nothing. They said it was for my own safety. This place bores me. Where are we?'

'Baghdad. Tell us about the bodies.'

The fellow had a tape-recorder.

'They had all been stabbed, in the heart or in the stomach. I didn't want to look. Besides, I was in the rear of the plane and I couldn't see much. That's what saved me. They killed the others, all of them except me, they forgot about me. Who are you?'

'Jack Moore. Associated Press. And you?'

'Luc. The name doesn't matter. I'm a journalist too, and I'm French. I've no next-of-kin to inform. Why are you smiling?'

Story ends. Tapping ends.

Luc sits back from the typewriter. He has just captured a dream. The dream of his return home after the death of Rasky, the dream of an adventure that misfired, a distorted view of a current happening, one of those fashionable obsessions that still titillate public opinion until they grow stale with familiarity. This time it was a dream of cold steel. The weapon check at the airport had been fruitless. So Luc stands up, turns his back on the desk and takes a few paces round the foreign realm of Rasky's apartment. He shrugs his shoulders. That's not a real adventure, is it? That's not it, an article for the press? Jack Moore had the face of Carlos. He was smiling. Rasky is going to die. And when he's dead, you'll quietly slip on a plane for Paris and carry on as before, playing the game as your own country

118

plays it. Top programme on television: *Fair Play*. Top panel game on television: *Answers for All*. And the country you dream about is one where the top programme would be called *Foul Play*, and the top panel game *No Answers*: all it needs is for someone to emerge who would be the champion of true understanding, a heroic earth-shattering idea that would put Justice back on her seat again and open up new spheres for Thought. No matter how much you write, you will never make anything happen in your life. And if anything did, you would never notice it. For that is the meaning of the dream you have trapped in your typed furrows of print. A writing-machine. Adventure will have brushed you aside, that's all. When his own anguish seems commonplace, a solitary writer of to-day can only concentrate on the cracks in the life around him. *Les dieux sont morts, adieu les vieux*. Adventure these days is penny-plain, not tuppence-coloured. So the solitary writer dreams up tales of imagination, perfect or almost perfect crimes: he is playing safe. In the vain belief that one day he will do better. He has been swallowed up by newspapers, magazines, television, and a world that overdoes everything. He plays safe till the day when fiction overhauls him. Death sometimes loses patience with the scribblers that cling to her apron-strings. Then she strikes. And the weapon she wields is cold steel, out of the blue. Luc smiles and leaves his text rolled on the typewriter. He can see inside himself more clearly now: see into his own dark night. Writing can no longer bring salvation. 17.15: Rasky is waiting for him.

Chapter Nineteen

Rasky. 'When people stop loving each other, everything becomes more exciting. It's the moment we all watch out for, eager as we are for things to happen. And we provoke our break-ups ourselves, if we have to. Close the door, will you? No-one but you must hear what I'm about to say, what I've been going over in my mind again and again, so as not to forget it. What I want to pass on to you. Come in, Luc, you've kept me waiting, come closer, I was afraid it was all going to slip from my memory. Listen.'

'We always think of death as being picturesque. We believe it imbues every human being with unsuspected courage and splendour. And we always think it's meant to provoke seizures of conscience and spurts of confession, and confronts you with the blinding truth. In my case, I've nothing essential to tell you, nothing to deliver, nothing to offer. You refuse everything anyway. This morning the doctor announced that they would stop giving me injections. Because I was so much better, he said. But I could read the truth in his face. I know how to read the underside of a lie, you know. An old habit of mine. I'm done for.'

'That's it, slip your hand round behind the pillow and massage the back of my neck. How do you manage to know how good that feels? It's good to do good. Don't stop. You've got rings under your eyes. Where did you go last night? What did you do? But no, don't tell me any more stories, I know the refrain. I've been singing it all my life. Perhaps you'd rather I told you what Carlos said to me, what Carlos did to me? Yesterday, while he was re-making the bed, he stripped to the waist to put me down, there, in the chair you're sitting in. I thought he was showing me his chest in order to seduce me, if he only knew . . . and then afterwards I told myself that he was only afraid he might dirty his jacket. Just as he was leaving, he let out that he was going to take a shower. My house of cards collapsed. So I started to imagine that I was the tablet of soap he was using under the shower and that he took a firm hold on me and slid me over his body, round his neck, through his hair and then over his face, like a grubby child who's been playing too hard and wants to look nice for a birthday dinner. Then, soapy and slippery in the palm of his hand, I slid under his armpits, through valleys of hairy thickets, and right down his arms to his fingers, the nails, and over the long clear lines in his hands, which I had never had the time to read. Then I discovered his stomach with broad circular movements, skirting his navel, then all round it again and again, till I slipped and slithered to the floor. Carlos picked me up. I evaded his grasp and he took hold of me again. This time I was lost in his crotch, lathering, drowning in a foam of tenderness, polishing the stones and stroking the muscle; then, bending forward, with a gesture he passed me through to the other place and there I go bobbing and scrubbing. Then come the legs, the knees and the feet and between the toes, the most delicious treat. He lays me down on the soap-dish. Forgets all about me. I can see him rinsing down. He is rubbing his chest. He has abandoned me. He doesn't know that I came to spy on him. He dries himself. Then he goes out, closing the shower-room door. I wanted to tell you, I needed to tell you that. It's all I know about him. Imagination.'

'Don't move. That's right. Let me feel the weight of my head in your hand. I'm amazed how heavy it is. That's a feeling which still makes some sense to me. They've stopped feeding me properly. They give me sugar dissolved in water, and sweet things taste bitter to me now. All my sensations and all the parts I ever dreamed of playing have been reversed. I always imagined a sudden death, a picturesque one, and I'm only allowed this interminable demise, this final one-man-show that goes on and on. And you're a kind spectator, too polite to leave before the end. You won't leave before it's all over. I was about to say that at least you owe me that. But you don't owe me anything. Not a thing. You have to stay because of all I owe *you*.' Smile. 'You see, I can still smile. It's all that's left me, apart from my eyes. Look at me. Close your eyes. Open your eyes. Close your eyes. It has just occurred to me that we forgot to make love together even once with our eyes shut, each one keeping his gratification a secret from the other. When we watched one another for every reaction, we concealed everything from each other. Yes, now I'm discovering this strange paradox in all my relationships, with everything and everyone. It's a bit late in the day to find out. But I suppose that's the really picturesque side of a final rendezvous. Are you listening?'

'Look at my body, what I've turned into. Yet while you're cupping the back of my neck in your hands, don't forget that in this head an adolescent is still making plans for the future, an adolescent who refuses to see himself as he is now. He thinks he's still on active service and arrogantly believes that he can take on anything: the little skirmishes of love, cruises by night, someone you pick up on a boulevard, who comes back home with you, get undressed and gives himself up to the game of give and take. It's natural for your body to leave you in the lurch, bugger off or break down. Something in the machine conks out and nothing works any more. That's a fine way to die. I've been treated to a flabby death, and serve me damn well right. But if my body lets me down, my mind has not deceived me. I am what I have chosen to be. And inside my head I'm still eighteen years old, the age you were when I met you. And today we are still both eighteen. Always the same age. When you feel the first stirrings of love. It's

123

my body that no longer relates. That's all. You're not listening any more.'

'A parasite devoured by parasites, a fine programme, isn't it? Right? You don't say a word. You're not even smiling. What if I told you that after that dream of the soap, I've lost all desire to discover Carlos, to see him really naked, completely in the nude: I know him off by heart. I've been all round him. A museum of youth I'm familiar with. I've visited it before, a hundred, a thousand times. Each time I used to leave you, it was to surprise myself with bodies different from yours, and all those other bodies brought me back to you: I still didn't really know you and I always had a kind of curiosity, an unfailing urge to look at you and watch you and discover you. This morning I told myself that I really must, at least once, tell you about my love for you. What a nasty big word! Tell you what it is that has bound me to you, and you to me. There was a curious look in your big brown eyes too, when you saw me coming back to you. Patient. Placid. Sure of yourself. I'd be back! And I was. This love of ours was simply a feeling of ease in danger, endangered by my capricious game of farewells. They followed a rhythm which matched our bouts of curiosity. I had found a way for us never to use each other up. Why should I feel guilty today, confessing that? Or you either, now it's all over? Let us admit that we enjoyed our sex together and that each time was like the first time. And that the only thing the jealous poaching queens in our world of men really resented was this perennial curiosity of ours and the strength of its renewal, our little game of I-go-I-come-back which always enabled us to evade capture by the enemy, time. Thank you, Luc, thank you.'

'You see, I'm crying. I've never been able to take them seriously, other people's tears. But mine today are scalding me. You'll see, they'll leave their trace behind. In furrows. As if my eyes were putting their tongues out. Tongues of fire. Kiss me.'

Luc bends over Rasky. Rasky looks astonished, startled. 'You're just out of school, you're just out of school and I'm waiting for you.' Luc presses his lips to Rasky's. Lips that no longer seem the same. They have a different taste. 'You see, you're afraid. So just look at me, that's all, let us kiss with our eyes.' Luc wipes Rasky's tears away. 'Watch out, you'll scald yourself.' Rasky smiles. 'Oh, if only I could have really stolen you away, run off with you, ravished you or whatever, abducted you, say. Yet the more I regret it, the more I tell myself that at one go I'd have ruined everything. We would never have travelled this long road together, side by side, pretending to go off and disappear and then coming back with our arms loaded with presents and our heads stuffed with desires. I don't know what else to say to you: I'm glad you're here today. I'm going to stop and lie down in the ditch. And you, keep going. You must keep going on. But at least we'll have travelled the road, all our road together. That's what it is, our love, the love we've both shared. Perhaps we're the only two who can understand that. We've put a great deal of honesty into that word, everything we had. And that's quite a lot. A lot better than a lie, because this way time has lost out. Look into my eyes, look!' Silence. Rasky's voice has grown hoarse, almost inaudible. He is going to sleep. In the palm of Luc's hand his neck has grown crushingly heavy. 'Go away, Luc, it's late and I don't want to see you any more . . .'

Chapter Twenty

Scalding hot coffees. Escape from reality. At Carpentras the shutters slammed shut at bedtime: in New York City there are no shutters. The windows have had their wings clipped. Startled looks, rigid facades, the good nature of an inhuman city, a federation of soliloquys. A purge of nice little words: out of the question. Mister Jack is waxing his moustache. Luc is sitting on a bench facing Sutton Hospital. He is counting the storeys. Rasky's either there or there. Luc has his pockets full of a crazy collection of marbles. He counts them again and again. Which is which? Scalding coffee. The bartenders are Greek: *Yassou. Ti kanis. Kala*? *Polykala*? *Malaka*! Luc orders a black coffee and a pizza. He'll drink his coffee black, without milk, without anything, *nature*. And the coffee in the carton mug is boiling. He has to wait. Slowly, very slowly consume the pizza and watch the heat spiral up from the coffee and disperse. Being in a hurry he wets his lips and burns himself, and the bartenders giggle. All he had to do was add milk and sugar and stir it with a plastic stick. In New York City if you like the liquid black you burn the tip of your tongue. And as the bartenders watch you they pass the word around: '*pusti*', pansy. So what?

Escape from reality. 'Do I dig your pullover! I just wanted you to know, it's so beautiful! Where'd you find it?' 'Paris.' 'Now I guess I know why!' The butch kid is munching his hamburger next to Luc, talking with his mouth full. 'I love beautiful things, they help me escape from reality.' Another dollop of ketchup and he's biting into a giant dill pickle. 'Don't you agree with me?' Luc answers with an evasive yes, then he pays and leaves. 'See you.' 'See you . . .'

The shutters were being slammed at Carpentras: Lucy is falling asleep on her bed. A little soft music, a honey-sweet cigarette, and at the back of her memory the sound of evening just after dinner when the shutters are being closed, slammed shut, and one is glad to feel that one's at home and letting everyone know it. Madame Roussel is bringing the chair in from the balcony. 'It's going to rain tonight, I'll put another blanket on your bed.' Today, lying on her bedspread of fur, Lucy gazes at the shutterless picture windows of her bedroom and that great sky brooding over the city, a sky that is darkening into night. Everyone leads his own little life apart. When one is alone, no charge for surplus baggage.

Startled looks: all the skyscrapers round Central Park gape at it frozen in fascination, like owls round the rim of a well. At nightfall they don't even fly away. A thousand staring eyes, and soon a thousand lights. Staring at the happenings in the Park. That is all. It is enough for them. Stuffed birds.

Rigid façades: 'This vertical city excites me.' The good nature of an inhuman city: it plays the part of an inapproachable great lady, then all at once calls up a tree, a garden or a house with steps up to the entrance protected by an awning. Splendidly overpowering, suddenly it scales itself down to a pedestrian's level. Walk, don't walk, green light, red light, yellow taxis: here there is a world of automobiles (tyres screeching round bends, the bell-like sound of ill-fitting manholes, bing, bong, a passing car, bing, bong, there's another, a truck, a bus . . .) and a world of pedestrians (vote for Olivieri, I am Olivieri, I want to stand again as your Senator, here, read this, thank you, people pass in the street, evading or inviting each other's eyes, it's the exodus from the office blocks. Carlos is getting Rasky ready for the night, hello and then good-night).

A federation of soliloquys: Rasky's life, Luc's life Lucy's life and so on. Every human being is an embryonic text, a linear track of solitude yearning for a crossing of the ways. Every human being is an exercise-book, ripped up, torn to shreds, of no use. But this is not a *chanson triste*. Cities are full of trees that are dead or on reprieve. It is all too much for them, too much rank air to breathe. Yet meanwhile the Earth goes on turning, the Earth doesn't give a damn. Though at times she feels sad and wonders if there's something unexpected she could do. Turn a bit more slowly or spin round the other way, so that every human being is a little less sure of things and even starts doubting whether anything belongs to him at all. Every human being talks to himself, soliloquizes. So one starts out with the story of one's life, going one's own sweet way, weaving a pattern of refusals and denials embroidered with one's choices and one's joys. Then comes the day when one decides that this earth must contain at least one other human being ready to lend an ear and launch a dialogue. So one stops talking to oneself, one addresses other people. And one starts off with an S-M nib, a lie-writing machine or a myth-making fountain pen whose speciality is farewell letters. One lays oneself down on a bed of paper sheets, and one gives and sells oneself for love. 'And now, Ladies and Gentlemen, you must realise that New York is only a pretext. Now, Ladies and Gentlemen, you must tell us about your ever-changing cyclorama, that unfortunate stage on which throughout your life you put on the same self-centred spectacle. With no-one in the auditorium and the programme-sellers on strike. They're on hunger strike, the show has folded, adventure is no longer flown from the rigging loft of the city and the earth is nothing but a big town, one big ghetto if you like, crowded with people muttering, chanting the story of their life.' Listen to their soliloquys.

A purge of nice little words: remove from the written text every 'isn't it', every 'and so', every useless little cog in the machine. Strip the text down, give it freedom, vigour and

129

resilience, polish the words, throw out the lightweight if decorative almonds and just keep the petits-fours which can still spring a surprise. Pull the string of the text so taut that it could sever your fingers. Ping, the text snaps. It is the end. That was some book, Ladies and Gentlemen. Three dramas in three bedrooms: a white one in Sutton Hospital, a green one in the Veronese Suite, and a dusty one full of scurbius where Odette is vacuum-cleaning—Monsieur Luc may be coming home soon. Three bedrooms, three bodies, and it's not take it or leave it, but take it again and again. Once you agree to let the magic of a book take you out of yourself, you have to carry on to the end. Even if the city is no more than a backdrop. Even if no-one talks to anyone else.

Mister Jack is waxing his moustache: business is going well. But what will he have to think up next, after this?

Rasky is there, in his room. Carlos has wedged the chair against the door. He has removed his jacket. He has opened his fly. He is doing what he must. Perhaps because he wants to as well. Rasky is thinking that it's just like his dream and yet not nearly so good. Too clean. The soap got there first. Deodorant. Rasky has always liked a man to smell like a man. Odour, a genuine odour would bring him to life again: *miracolo!*

Luc has his pockets full of a crazy collection of marbles, glass and clay ones and motley alley taws as big as Mirabelle plums. If he cheats, he loses, and then he'll be late for lunch. Coming out of school. The day will arrive when there'll be someone waiting for him. Meanwhile he plays. He has forgotten the rules, the order of things. He simply knows he has to aim well and shoot, and substitute one marble for another within the triangle near the wall. In which case he earns the right to a second go. To have two lives! And then he will win enough miniature planets to burst his pockets. Or else he will lose and suffer the tortures of a *Deus* with no *Machina*. On his way home (scent of the horse-chestnut in flower, the delights of the Boulevard d'Argenson, unveiling of the bust of Saint-Exupéry, speeches and little French flags) he will call at the baker's and ask for a hot roll. And when he gets home he won't be feeling hungry any more. During the lunch-hour he will count his marbles. Luc dreams of the day when he will forget all this, his childhood. The sheets of oblivion are black. Sheets of paper are white, and then blue. To embark on the great voyage of writing. To deliver oneself. Or deliver oneself up manacled to the militiamen of death. The first days of October, a day, an evening no different from any other. As he walks Downtown, Luc is thinking that he too, if he'd tried, might have written the book that could have saved mankind. But why he *too*? Has anyone else ever done it? Who? He shrugs his shoulders. Now Rasky can snuff it if he must: nothing counts but the trucks.

Chapter Twenty-One

'In the summer,' said Carlos, 'I have one weekend out of three off duty. Three days at a time. So I treat myself to the luxury train, the Blue Arrow. You have to make a reservation at least two months in advance. I get off at Southampton and go to see my Mom. She does house-cleaning there. When folks are on vacation in the summer, she works real hard. In the winter, she just keeps the keys to all the houses. Then she writes me a bit more often.' Carlos had opened the door of the room. Rasky had asked him to. 'I've got the feeling there's some wind from outside coming in through the corridor,' he had said, 'I know it's only an impression but talk to me, tell me about your life.' Carlos had sat down, not *in* the armchair, but on the arm. 'The nurses would get jealous, they'd spread it around, and there's no point asking for trouble.' Legs outstretched, Carlos is leaning slightly forward, with one foot crossed over the other and his hands folded over his stomach. 'Be careful,' said Rasky, 'you might slide off.' 'I'm used to it,' said Carlos. 'I know these armchairs like the back of my hand. I could almost call them by their first names.' Irony. Rasky had the impression that a shadow just passed in the corridor, a dark shadow holding a pair of slippers, ladies' slippers, black ones, with pink ribbons to make them less scary. Sweet death. 'And this Blue Arrow thing, it would make a fantastic film. You want to hear the story?' 'Go ahead, Carlos, tell me.' 'Well then, the last weekend in August I had a seat in the parlor car of the Blue Arrow. A coach reserved for late-comers, or for people like me who can't afford a private compartment. It's a sort of old-fashioned train, you know. Like a Victorian drawing-room inside, with big club armchairs and little black boys to serve the drinks and offer you the choice of twenty different brands of cigar. Really living it up. It's all I want to help me forget the corridors of this hospital.' Carlos smiled. 'That particular day I'd had a few drinks while waiting for the train. I felt great. Completely detached. I watched whoever it was coming in, sitting down, and who was watching who, and I tried to imagine what each of their lives was like. I noticed there wasn't a woman among them. In the summer, of course, all their families have gone to the coast. The husbands just spend the weekends. Fine-looking poppas, decent family men, in their thirties. Genuine American middle-class. Clean-living. With gleaming teeth and impeccable grins, all in suits that are badly cut but magnificent cloth. Colour of the tie a bit too gaudy, but with a casual air to carry it off. Well, while I've got them under observation, I come to realise that they're all in love with each other. They all desire one another. There's something in the looks they exchange, and there are about thirty of us in the parlor car, that's not just due to the usual boredom and inactivity of a journey by train: they look at each other because they want one another. They don't talk to each other because they're all jealous, envying and desiring one another, but behind their newspapers they're making love, a sidelong glance as they turn the pages, and as they light their cigarettes and swallow a mouthful of gin they stare hard at the guys who face them or who sit across the way. A furious platonic game that lasts the whole length of the trip. And no-one ever speaks to anyone, or very little. A remark about the weather, have you any matches, didn't we see each other last weekend, it never goes further than that. They're married men. And at Southampton their wives are waiting for them on the station platform. And that's the great scene in the film. They embrace their wives lovelessly. Coldly. Mechanically. You know what I mean? Can you see it? But the kids are there too. And they kiss their children joyfully. They bend at the knees and pick them up in their arms. What do you think?' 'It's a nice idea, but have you thought of a title?' 'At first I thought of *The Blue Arrow*. Then one day in the paper I saw the photograph of a painting they'd refused to show in a Modern Art Exhibition, oddly enough at Southampton. This "painting" was really a blown-up photograph of lips, shown vertically. At once, you see, it looked more like a cunt, a pussy, a vagina. So back to the arrival of the train. The artist had decided to call his picture *Band in Southampton*. And I thought that it would make a good title for my story.' Carlos folded his arms and wagged his head. 'Only trouble is, I don't know how to write. I'd have to make a novel of it first and then a scenario, and that all scares me. Not my scene.' Silence.

The odour of Carlos' skin: how could Rasky ask his nurse not to take a shower for at least two days? Odour restored! Smothered in ointment, aseptic, flabby, abandoned, even deprived of the power to do what he would with his own body, now having its revenge on Rasky for the time he had gambled so recklessly away as he hoped in the fury of this futile dissipation to summon up the magic of a meeting, a partnership, and stumbled on his parallel relationship with Luc, who gave a fillip to his life, today all Rasky longs for is an odour, an authentic odour, one odour at last in this hygienic labyrinth of rooms and corridors. Whiteness is nothing. 'What are you thinking?' 'About your film.' 'No, you're thinking about something else, you're hiding something from me.' 'Yes, I was thinking about you.' Carlos comes up to the bed and strokes Rasky's brow. 'Relax, relax baby!'

'The hero, you know, should be a banker, filthy rich. About forty. And he'd be gazing at two guys sitting opposite, younger than him, two guys staring at each other who don't dare say a word. Then he'd remember an incident during the last war, identical, in an army truck

135

in the Ardennes. And then another, when he was a kid, in the bus he used to take to school. Stuff like that. And you'd see into his past, a whole past of failure to admit the truth. He's been a spectator all his life, of incidents like that, identical. The blind and stubborn way men go looking for companionship, the bond of man to man, each on an equal footing. Something to take their minds off that perfect wife who belongs to them and depends on them for everything. And when they embrace their children on the station platform, it is their champions they're embracing, potential victors in a match which *they* have lost. You understand?' Rasky gives a slight nod of the head. 'One day maybe these children will alter the time-table, they may even alter the sort of relationship their fathers have failed to create in the train. Yes, those poppas on the station platform at Southampton are embracing something they have lost: audacity. The Blue Arrow: thirty seats for thirty lonely men.' Silence. Carlos gently shrugs his shoulders. 'I know I was a bit drunk that day, but I like that story of mine, it tells me something . . .'

Concerning the unzipped fly: 'What I did just now was just what you expected of me, just what the look in your eyes was asking for. You see, I'm no different from anyone else, I'm made the same way as all the others. But there, it's exactly what you wanted, at the precise moment I did it. Correct?' Rasky closed his eyes. 'I'm right, aren't I?' Rasky opened his eyes, then closed them again. 'Come on, it's time to get you cleaned up. And no injection, as the Doctor said to stop them.' Carlos closed the door of the room. 'Want some music? O.K., no music.' Silence. 'Want the T.V.? O.K., no T.V.' Silence. 'I like your moods. You amuse me. I think you're a bit crazy, but I like crazy people. I like Rasky. You don't mind if I call you Rasky, do you?' Rasky never made any distinction between true and false affection, no doubt because affection is essentially false, it's an elegant way of holding other people at arm's

136

length, keeping them far enough away for them not to embarrass you. Affection is an embellishment of words and gestures which shuts you out at the precise moment when you appear to be made welcome. Leave your own circle and come into mine, leave your own world and come into mine, I'll show you my log-cabin at the far end of the park. My parents never go inside. I've never invited anyone else before. Come, and I'll show you. Childhood is a ball and chain we drag around with us till our very last moment. Carlos is talking to himself. Rasky has stopped listening. When Carlos lifts him up to set him down in the chair, Rasky imagines that the chest his face is pressed to suddenly opens like a dolomite rock delivering the sword that will allow him to finish himself off. Hara-kiri. Meanwhile, what is Luc doing now? Till his very last moment Rasky will be torn between the imperturbable schoolboy and that fine Utopia where men unzip their flies and offer themselves good-naturedly. 'That's it really, isn't it?'

Chapter Twenty-Two

The bigger the city, the more the young men feel at home there. This is the biggest cradle Luc has ever known. Yet get lost in it. A cradle of corners of streets and avenues, with toy boxes all over the place and shady nooks where baby can go to sleep with his arms spreadeagled or held out-outstretched. Papa is there, tall as tall, with something sticking out in front of him. Everything starts again from scratch. It is raining and in a few seconds the city becomes human: it looks at its reflection and assesses its own beauty. The cradle is wet and Luc is happy. He exists.

He will take the Downtown road again, trudging through the rain. He will arrive there soaked, clammy, feverish. He will arrive behind the evening trucks ahead of all the others. He will wait there in a corner, sitting on an oil-drum with his feet on a pile of planks. He will watch the rain disturb the surface of the puddles. He will tap his fists against the palms of his hands, as though he'd messed up one appointment and was sure he'd miss out on the next. What had Rasky meant when he left him? 'Go away, Luc, I don't want to see you any more . . .' Was he to come back tomorrow or the day after? Or true to their pattern of parallel affinities, should he go on alone with hands in pockets and a truant conscience, never asking any more questions, with the vague remembrance of a friend he once met on the way, his travelling companion for nearly fifteen years? The rain fell twice as hard. Luc took cover under a truck and squatted down with his hands clasped under his chin. It is Saturday. He counts up the days, then works them out again, it's Saturday night all right, a time for rendezvous of all kinds. Everyone's out. Cramp.

Luc shifts his position. A handsome negro comes and crouches next to him. He stuffs a popper up his nose, then holds it out to Luc, who contemplates the two-pronged capsule. Luc sticks it into his nose like a plug into a socket and inhales ferociously. The effect is instantaneous: the city becomes a pin-cushion spinning round in the troubled sky of the puddles. And the raindrops turn into bloodstains. Beneath the truck the ground is hard and dry: Luc lies full length. The guy crawls right up against him, opening his jacket, bare-chested. Luc pinches his nipples, two large pieces of confetti, pink against the black skin. 'Harder!' Luc bites them. The guy groans, with his left hand undoes Luc's clothing and plants one prong of the popper in Luc's nostril. 'Go on, have a good sniff!'

The truck, childhood, that gigantic piano which Luc would hide under with his special treats, a lump of cane sugar or a piece of quince cheese, on Thursday afternoons when he was bored, with all his lessons learnt and all his homework done, and it was raining and the visit to the Musée Carnavalet was off and Maman would ask Nanny where Luc was. 'I don't know, Madame.' Luc was hiding under the piano, in the drawing-room under the piano, that musical coffin on which nobody played, forsaken, out of tune, a memorial in a room for the living. Luc hid there with his afternoon snack. At school he was a good pupil. A well-behaved child. On the day of his First Holy Communion the chaplain gave him an art-book, *The Shrine of Saint Ursula*, fifteen reproductions in colour, with the following inscription on the fly-leaf: 'For Luc, who I am sure will always be as good as these pictures.' Pictures of fire, of pin-cushions, blood and martyrdom. Luc was to tear out the fly-leaf and then hide the beautiful book so that no-one should ever know what it was that he secretly refused and desired. Pictures of towns going up in flames...

The guy slaps Luc. 'Hey, man!' He is biting Luc's ear and Luc grasps him by the hair and twines himself round him. With concertinaed trousers masking their shoes and their clothes scattered about they lie face to face, outspread hand clamped on outspread hand, and they kiss as if kissing their own image in a mirror. Poppers again. Luc pulls himself up and bangs his head against the steel casing of this travelling piano. He is bleeding. The other guy licks the graze on his forehead. Luc is not sure whether he has hurt himself or whether it is his heart that has leapt into his head and is drumming a tattoo. He lies flat and the guy takes him like a woman, from the front, gently, very gently. Canoeing down the Mississippi. Watch out, don't rock the boat or it's going to capsize in that river of rain. This time Luc shuts his eyes, he no longer belongs anywhere. He can feel this boy on top of him, plunging. And the boy puts a yellow pill on Luc's tongue. 'Come on, swallow it, get that saliva flowing and swallow.' Silence. 'Come on, come on!' The fellow braces his back. With one fingertip he strokes the wounded brow, there under the piano that hides you and kills. And wounds. 'If the truck moved off, if the truck ran over me, I'd be a puddle.'

Caresses. Afterwards. The guy lights a cigarette. He rolls his jacket into a ball and slips it under Luc's neck. Luc opens his eyes. Crouching all round them, new arrivals are taking everything in. Motionless. Scared. Dazed. Conniving. Speechless. The great *soirée* is about to begin. Luc feels his trouser pockets. He has lost his keys, his wallet. Now he cannot even raise a smile. He lies back. His partner licks his navel, then all round it in ever-widening circles. Every now and again he moistens his tongue and then resumes. Concentric circles. Luc feels himself swept into the vortex. Hudson. Deep waters in the Port of New York. Black waters. Negro.

Chapter Twenty-Three

Trying it on. Lucy gets up and hunts for her watch: midnight. She is hungry and calls Kenneth to ask him to order a hamburger from the snack-bar on 58th Street. 'He's not here this week-end, Lady. This is Billy, what do you want?' 'Nothing. Nothing, thanks.' Billy has a large pimple on his nose. Lucy doesn't want him to come up. 'I have nothing in common with him.' In the kitchen, crude light and an empty ice-box. Just milk. She drinks some milk. And munches a few crusts of toast which she goes on chewing in the hope that eventually they will leave a sweet taste in her mouth. But the taste never comes. She spits the bread out in the garbage can. Bitter bread. Her unlucky day. Pepper.

Lucy slams back the sliding doors of the closet for clothes. Grey, nothing but grey, and hanging right at one end in a see-through bag, the green dress, her dress, her 'débutante' costume. Lucy walks round the apartment, switching on all the lights, lovingly stooping over every lamp. This evening she is entertaining, music and champagne. One bottle, overlooked in the rack at the back of the refrigerator, ice-bucket and three glasses please, Mademoiselle Lucienne. Three. Everything is ready. Lucy slips the dress on and twirls around, gasping with delight and flinging out her arms. Barnaby greets her at the entrance to the apartment. She gives him her arm. He pays her the famous compliment about the green dress. She is radiant, she has brought it off. Sulking on the sofa, Lammert is waiting his turn. 'He's studying', murmurs Barnaby. 'He's very sweet,' answers Lucy. 'Tell me about Carpentras, that's it, talk to me about Carpentras!'

A chaste dress bordering on the knee, a transparent dress revealing just as much as it should to be seductive. The fragrance of Kenya, the scent of wood and tropical forests, a gentle stroll through the garden. 'Have no fear. Let them say what they want, it's *our* birthday this evening. Would you like me to say all the right words for the occasion? *Amour, toujours*, that's what it should be in French, isn't it? *Amour, toujours.* No, don't move, I want to look at you, just as you are. What a lot of business I've had with your Embassy lately! It was almost like droppng in on friends. On the French of all people!' Lucy serves the champagne. Clinks glasses. Accepts one invitation to dance, then another, moony fox-trots. 'What's this, Lammert, not drinking?' 'I'm watching you, Madame, just watching.'

A ring at the door. Billy: 'I've brought you two hamburgers. Ain't that what you wanted, Lady? Don't be afraid to ask.' 'Thank you, Billy, thank you.' 'You look swell tonight, Lady.' 'Thank you, Billy, thank you.' Lucy wastes no time shutting the door, but when she returns all her guests have gone and the green dress feels a bit tight round the waist. She has put on weight. Three glasses on the table, one empty, two full.

Lucy opens the little package and uncovers the two hamburgers, which are still warm. Testing them with her finger, she grasps the one on the left with both hands and bites into it. Tasteless meat, insipid white bread. She spits out the first mouthful. On the coffee-table in front of the large couch lies an unfinished jig-saw puzzle 'Adam and Eve', Adam on one side, Eve on the other. On the cover of the box there is a photograph of them fully clothed, but the two-sided jig-saw eventually uncovers them in their more primitive finery. Naturally Lucy had started on the Adam side. And she had begun with his genitals. Disappointment, an insignificant little thing, a little American Queen Kong affair. A model-boy, hairy, sprouting hair from top to toe, so that several times she had mistaken a piece of the thigh for the hair on his head. Gradually, over a period of three weeks, she had revealed the man's body, the outline of the belly, the folds above the navel, the gentle blur of the shoulders merging into the dark background, the smile on the lips split into four pieces (the fourth one particularly hard to find) and above all the feet, the angle of them, the stance, and the equilibrium they gave to the whole body. A real man for you! At first she was greedy. She had to find out at once 'how he was built'. Then slowly this feeling gave place to a different urge. Every part and parcel of the body had a strange way of overlapping, each piece leading on to the next. She trained herself to recognise the slightest variation in the skin, and in every piece by the sheen and reflecting glints of a single hair the probable direction of its growth: then she slotted it in. She had always thought of jig-saw puzzles as a waste of time. Sheer futility. But with this puzzle she put the clock back. She re-created an image. The image of a man. But his torso was unfinished. The shaded areas were too hard to sort out. And below his left nipple the pieces for the heart were still missing. So Lucy began to set aside all the black pieces which made up the outside of the puzzle, easy to distinguish because of the straight edge. Then she started collecting all the pieces that showed a patch of skin, however minute, on either side of the puzzle. So one by one she inspected every single piece in order to make a final choice between those on which the shaded flesh was masculine, Adam-like and hairy, and those with soft shadows, pools of ice-cool Eve-like flesh. When everything was in order, Adam's portrait was still crying out for the pieces that made up his heart. She checked all the male pieces and tried them out; none of them fitted. She rubbed her eyes and started again. A record was spinning round soundlessly. Kneeling there in her green dress, she would crease it. But nothing could distract her now: Adam is smiling, asking for her help. Small members sometimes spring a big surprise. And *vice versa*. Lucy smiles and bites her lips. She is amused at her reflections. She goes on with the game. Mister Jack won't telephone tonight; two nights running, that's impossible. So she devotes herself to this other corpse, the picture. There in the middle the pieces are missing; but that's it, of course! Some of the pieces *are* missing, she assures the salesman, so I'm bringing this puzzle back, there are some missing pieces, for three weeks I've been hunting for them . . . Then Lucy reminds herself that this is the general rule: you *always* have the impression that there is one piece missing, and then after a thorough search you find it and you realise it was there all the while, though you'd tried it time and time again! That's how it is, I never had enough faith in the way it was cut. I never looked closely enough. Lucy gets up, walks round the table, changes the record, strokes her hair, smoothes out the skirt of the green dress and bends over the puzzle again. 'I *must* find it.' She searches, tries various pieces out. She cannot find the pieces for the heart. She falls asleep on the floor beside the couch. She dreams that Adam is eating hamburgers, crumpling the paper cartons into little balls, then playing with them and dancing and holding out his arms to her. He says nothing. He speaks to her with his hands. Where his heart should be there is a gaping hole. And then she is frightened and hides under the table. Curls herself up small and shuts her eyes very tight. And very tightly the night closes the gates of its sexuality around her. Lucy is off on a beautiful trip. Black.

Chapter Twenty-Four

Negro is sitting cross-legged. Luc is sprawling in front of
him, his head resting between the other fellow's legs, the
back of his neck against his fly. It is still raining. The truck
makes a curious canopy, which could start in New York
and finish in the inner suburbs of Mexico City: the biggest
truck in the world, the biggest Big Top on earth, the Lucus
Sexus Circus and its whipping pricks, a new show every
half-hour. It is played out on a north-south axis, in the
recumbent position, the head clamped between the folded
legs of the other creature, the black-jacketed scurbius
with its black penis and shiny black skin. Negro, chocolate
blackamoor: coarse-grained, vanilla-scented skin, lips
like little cushions of tender flesh, a body veiled for a
funeral. The ceremony is beginning. Crawling, on their
knees, or with their legs upright but bending at the waist,
arms hanging limply or jerking into action, here come the
robots, the others, the voyeurs, visitors to the interminable
truck, a steel umbrella which could cover the whole earth.
But what was that yellow pill which grows and grows inside Luc's head, exploding into a thousand colours,
distorting the world with its firework display? Luc is naked,
but who has removed his trousers, his shoes and socks?
Who is sucking at his toes, first one mouth, then two, then
three? He wants to buck and wriggle and break the hold
these mouths have on the Downtown end of his body, but
the sensation is too acute, the sweetness of it too much like
pain, too intense for him to take evasive action. He plays
dead. Pretends that nothing is happening. Negro's knees
are squeezing his shoulders, crushing him; he can hardly
breathe, a fine mess, there'll be nothing left of him, he

knows that, and the thought of it overwhelms him. Bye-bye to the dolly boys of Paris, the lonely gropers of the Tuileries, the gigolos of the Pincio and the tea-room trade of the Tivoli Gardens. The trucks of the United States are the biggest trucks in the world. They breed men like insects and the elite is hatched out on Saturday and Sunday nights. They lay their eggs when it's raining. And they do it on a patch of wasteland when the earth is dry, with puddles near at hand so the grubs will have something to drink. The congregation has gathered, worshippers shaking their left wrists. And they spit in your eye and all over. Downtown.

'Oh, cool it!' Negro waves them off. They move aside and make room. He puts Luc's socks on again, pulling them tight over Luc's feet, each gesture slow and deliberate, with a gleam of passion that flares up in Luc's mind and dazzles him. 'Don't move, I'll take care of you.' He pulls Luc's trousers back on. 'Fuck off, leave us alone.' His voice sounds far away, hoarse, velvety, dusky, at one and the same time rasping and caressing. Luc tries to get up but a shaft of light nails him to the ground. 'Police!' The glare of headlights, the thrill of fear, dispersal and flight. Negro flattens himself over Luc. 'Don't move.' The squad car remains facing the trucks for a long, a very long time, long enough to drive out of one's mind all memory of history books and wars and fine mornings on the way to school when you don't feel like going but you go all the same and through the classroom window gaze at the sky that is pretending to be the sea with islands of cloud and currents of wind and men drowning unseen. 'Don't move.' The squad car turns around. No-one left under the trucks but Luc and Negro. 'Help me, they'll be back.' Luc slips on his shirt and buttons it up. The wrong buttons. He undoes them and does them up again. 'O.K.?' 'O.K., hurry!' Negro ties up Luc's shoelaces. 'What got into you, wearing shoes with laces, *here*!' They crawl out behind the

148

trucks as the others begin to creep back. 'My name's Andrew, what's yours?' 'Luc.' 'Luck?' 'No, Luc, without a K at the end, I'm French.' Luc has the feeling that someone else has answered for him, another self. 'Come on.' In places Luc's shirt is sticking to his chest. In places Luc's trousers are sticking to his legs. 'Here,' says Andrew, 'here's your keys, a good thing you've got me with you.' Luc shrugs his shoulders, takes the keys and puts them in the left pocket of his jacket. 'I saw the guy who stole your billfold. Did you have much with you?' Luc shrugs his shoulders. 'Come on, we'll get a drink in here. Gay bar.' In the rest-room Luc strips to the waist. He dries his shoulders and his stomach with paper towels. He spits in the wash-basin, soaks his face, fills his mouth with water and spits again and again. Then he puts his shirt on, pushes open the door of a W.C. behind him, lowers his trousers and wipes the slime from his legs, that spittle of rain and larvae, those tears from under the trucks. There is no lock on the door. Someone pushes at it. 'Wait.' 'It's Andrew, every-thing O.K.?' 'O.K.' Latrines, a cul-de-sac, no exit. The wall carries a constellation of addresses and telephone numbers, a matter of discipline, lovers of bondage and leather and chains. Luc smiles. The first smile of the even-ing.

They are celebrating the anniversary of the bar. On a platform a coffin on which is written in large letters ONE MORE YEAR FOLKS. Flashing lights, fairground décor sprays of flowers and, hanging from their necks from the ceiling, strangled dolls, each one bearing the name of a rival establishment. The bartenders wear leather tee-shirts with the words: 'Mrs. Nixon is expected at any moment. Do her proud.' Andrew offers Luc a tankard of beer. 'You're crazy.' 'Which of us is the crazier?' Andrew pinches Luc's ear and strokes the back of his neck. 'I felt a bit scared, those guys were beginning to do just anything.' 'What's anything?' 'Well, they'd gotten out of control. I

149

don't trust those trucks. Still, you can trust me.' Silence. 'You do trust me, don't you?'

'My father's black, my mother's Puerto Rican. I have an Irish name, I'm a Baptist, and I work for a Jewish florist. And you're the first Frenchman I've ever met.' Andrew spoke in a dry tone. 'Listen', he says, pinching Luc's arm. The noise of steel-studded boots, the creak of leather jackets, the smell of badly tanned hide, sounds and smells battling together, bruised and battered faces, everyone waiting, lashing out at each other with their eyes. A night of brutality. 'I don't go for this dump, come on back to my place.'

80th Street, Westside. 'This is my ghetto,' Andrew admits, 'I love it and you're sure gonna love it too.' Andrew squeezes the words out through clenched teeth. 'Don't you know how to smile?' 'It makes me tired.' A ramshackle staircase with tall steps, steeply pitched. 'You go first.' 'Which floor is it?' 'Way up at the top, last door.'

Chapter Twenty-Five

You don't go down, you just go. When you create, all you do is salvage from the past. Only through the prism of the individual and his here-and-now can a fresh gloss be brought to events that time will sweep away and bury. A novel about three people unable to write their own, novels that were meant to save mankind and not just entertain, to sharpen mankind's curiosity and not just titillate by aiming below the belt or too far over everyone's head at those extinct gods of the Night Flight, or the Royal Road, gods who no longer sustain our blasé Terrestrials with the Fruits of the Earth. Nathanaël, lie down beside me and nestle up close, that's the style, let yourself go and receive my fond caresses in broad daylight: today a penis is a penis, stripped of all taboos, no more or less than a pendulous morsel of flesh that stiffens when stroked. Mankind is no longer concerned with salvation, all that men can do is face up to themselves and see themselves as they really are. When they have the courage to look themselves straight in the face. When some of them are mad enough to hold up a mirror which neither distorts nor beautifies nor tans the skin, a mirror that is merely a mirror, coldly reflecting. You don't go down any more, you walk straight ahead. Hell is there, right in front of you. For the solitary ones, no diversion is possible. A road with no exit, and then it's goodnight Lady Life, the champagne of the twentieth century has gone to your head. Yellow pill and poppers, one Big Trip to the Historical Costume Museum. Drop-outs with hearts of gold drop round you like flies. Without even having the time to think what they would really have liked to do or do better, like saving someone,

one person at least. A little tact, please. Explain yourself. Rasky is dreaming. He is sitting in a perambulator, propped upright in his dry nappies: he has not piddled yet, he hasn't been given his bottle. In front of him a promenade by the sea, a made-up path edged with gravel, empty benches, low tide and a hazy sun circled in mist. But who is pushing his pram, who? Rasky turns round: the hood over his head prevents him from seeing who is taking him out. He feels like crying but he knows he'd be punished: no sweet chocolate-flavoured milk. Mmmm, oh that lovely smell from a warm feeding-bottle! So Rasky sits up very straight, holding on to the oilcloth edge of the pram, and waits. The pram teeters onto the gravel, watch out, it's going to tip over. Rasky braces himself, no, no, behind him the propelling force pushes the pram back on the path. The wind rises from the sea, pungent and blistering. Rasky pulls a little face. At the end of the promenade, the asphalt path inclines steeply down to the beach. But who is holding on to Rasky's pram, who? The path becomes a rampart looking down on the sea, then a toboggan-slide, stretching down in a straight line to a point on the horizon where it meets the rising tide and its waves as high as houses. The pungent smell comes from down there. Who is holding Rasky back, who? All at once the propelling force lets go of the pram, which starts racing down the slope. Rasky doesn't cry out: his cry gets stuck in his throat. He is done for. There is laughter behind his back. Running footsteps which soon catch up with him. He is saved. Then released again, and the pram picks up speed as Rasky digs his baby fingers into the oilcloth round the edge of the carriage. He tries to scream, but no sound emerges from his open mouth, the wind drives a nail down his throat. Laughter and footsteps behind Rasky, the laughter peals out and then Phew! He is caught. Rasky hears diddums diddums, that refrain for cute little babies which Rasky does not like. He gets rocked in his pram, or

152

rather jolted to and fro, to and fro: then once more he is released. Again. But this time the slope outruns the laughter. No-one catches up with the pram, the laughs become shouts and soon the sound of the sea muffles the screaming as the pram gets swallowed in one mouthful by those waves as high as houses. Rasky hears the gurgling as bubbles shoot from his mouth and the fish brush past him. He awakes. He thinks he is in an aquarium. He is soaked in sticky sweat. He slides one finger onto the emergency bell next to his left hand. An open door and light. An unknown woman's face, a nurse with purple lips. 'Sorry, sir, the Doctor said not to give you any more injections. I can give you a compress or two if you like.' 'Where's Carlos?' 'He's off duty, sir. At this hour, you know. Besides, it's Saturday night . . .'

Lucy is dreaming about Lucienne. *Maman* is cooking the dinner. Lucy is sitting on the chair on the balcony. She is gripping the railings with both hands, rocking to and fro on the two back legs of the chair. Backwards and forwards, backwards and forwards, rubbing her head against the velvet sky and reciting tomorrow's lessons. Her mother has just arranged her hair into ringlets that tickle her neck, back and forth, back and forth, and next day the little Jewish girls in her Primary School will be jealous of her new coiffure and they'll pull her hair. Is it always best to belong to the camp of the majority? No, it works quite well as it is. Lucienne can look after herself: she comes out first all round. She is the little wonder-girl of the Primary School at Carpentras. Backwards and forwards. 'What are you doing?' 'I'm playing swings.' 'Take care you don't hurt yourself.' '*Oui, maman.*' Forwards: the passers-by look up. Backwards: the sky flushes and turns crimson, as the little girl stares it in the face. Forwards: a light has just appeared in the shop-window of the baker's where they make unleavened bread. Backwards: the sun has just gone down behind the crags of Montmirail, the shark's teeth, the comb of the River Rhône. Forwards, backwards, forwards: I'll be an air hostess and my head will go spinning round as it is now. Backwards: oh no I won't, up there it's too high up, so I'll just travel about with a string of hat-boxes. Hat-boxes with nothing inside but ribbons, ribbons to tie up my hair. My hat is my hair. 'Lucienne?' '*Oui, maman.*' 'Stop it!' '*Non, maman, non.*' The chair is creaking a bit, and the railings round the balcony feel ice-cold as the shadows creep into the street. Forwards: night down below, electric light. Backwards: night up above, a *petit point* of stars and a quartered moon like a yoke in the cloth of heaven. Forwards, backwards, forwards . . . and over you go! The railings give way and Lucienne is falling through space. She wants to cry for help, but the emptiness chokes her. She is falling, falling. That balcony was so high up in the sky: there's Carpentras, like a little dot down below. Lucienne is falling, her arms outstretched: she'd like to fly, but she can't. Birds try to swoop at her in their flight, tearing her schoolgirl apron and tugging her ringlets out. Oh, I won't look beautiful tomorrow! There's the town within jumping distance, the outer boulevards, my street, my house, the baker's shop with the unleavened bread and in front of it the manhole over the drains. *Maman* is shouting as she lifts up the cover: Lucienne falls right in, spinning round inside a spinal column with the vertebrae lit up from outside, then up she goes again to the back of the neck and the brain, and when she's gone through the brain, the skull. Crack, the skull splits like a nutshell between the hulls of two yachts. Lucy wakes with a start. Bangs her head on the edge of the coffee table by the couch. The green dress is all creased. Five o'clock in the morning. The city is asleep. Lucy casts a last look at the puzzle and goes to bed. She stumbles. Her head is spinning round. She has fallen from such a height!

Chapter Twenty-Six

The walls are leprous. Broad patches of yellowish paint
have scaled off. 'I don't even sweep it, I like it like this, I
like it to look neglected,' says Andrew, tossing his leather
jacket on the floor. Short-sleeved tee-shirt, ebony arms:
Luc remembers that book of strip cartoons which he had
read and re-read as a child. *The Adventures of Chocolate*,
the nice little black boy who wants to learn to read and
write, gets taken up by the Missionary Priest and finally
lands up in Paris where he feels cold, very cold, but where
a very rich old lady offers him a pullover and has suits
made for him out of old frock-coats that belonged to her
husband, who died in the war. So Chocolate becomes an
engineer, learns how to build dams and goes back to his
own country. His own village is doomed by the very first
dam he constructs (all alone?). The Missionary dies in his
arms and gives him his blessing. To be continued in our
next. 'Right, get moving.' 'I'd like to take a shower.' 'If
you want to, but there's no hot water.'
    Luc gets undressed. It is a huge room with a high ceiling
and over the fireplace a picture of Louis XIV on a prancing
horse. Pinned to the picture are photographs of Andrew,
naked, front view, back view, sprawling, in chains, and
with a sailor's cap on his head. 'Come on, move.' Socks
screwed into a ball left lying on the floor, dirty briefs and
threadbare shirts. 'Right, yeah, O.K., it's my mess, I like
it that way.' Luc is warily folding his blue jeans, then his
shirt and his socks. 'What the hell are you doing?' Andrew
snatches the clothes out of Luc's hands and hurls them to
the ground. Chocolate is getting cross. He grips Luc by

the shoulder. 'If you want that shower, buddy, get on with it!'

Luc crosses the bedroom. The bed is unmade, ravaged, filthy, quite filthy with stains all over. It is framed between two large wardrobes, like giant strong-boxes. Instead of a canopy over the bed, a mirror slung from the ceiling. 'Bathroom's in there.' Andrew is giving orders, pushing Luc at arm's length in front of him. 'What are you gaping at? You scared?' 'Those insects . . .' 'Oh, they're all over the place, gotta get used to them, man. The bathroom belongs to them.' Standing in the bath-tub Luc turns on the hot water and hears the empty pipes shudder and croak like someone vomiting. Andrew cuts it off. 'I told you, cold water, that's all.' And he turns that on. Luc is caught in a glacial jet. 'No soap: better just scrub yourself.' The water is green and then yellow, and the stink of chlorine fills the bathroom. Luc's hair gets plastered over his face and blinds him. The cold water beats down on the top of his head like hail and re-echoes inside him. He kneels in the bath: this time the powerful jet pins him down. It's raining pebbles. It seems to Luc as if the whole building is vibrating with him. Niagara. Chocolate is getting his own back. Chocolate has learned his lesson. Luc feels he'd like to claw off the discoloured enamel of the tub, but in the five days since he arrived in New York City he has conscientiously bitten his nails right down. He clenches his fists. Andrew stops the cold water. 'O.K., move, out! No towels, so you'll have to jump around.' Andrew takes hold of him and sets him on his feet. Luc mutters: 'What was that yellow thing you gave me just now?' 'Nothing, man, nothing, a fun thing.' 'Tell me,' murmurs the shivering Luc, 'tell me.' 'Happiness, buddy, happiness, and now we're going to have a ball.' 'No.' 'What d'ya mean, no? Come on . . .' Dripping wet, Luc stretches out on the bed. Andrew dries him with the dirty sheets. Luc is thinking how the dirt will make him filthy again. He closes his eyes. Lets it

156

happen. Andrew is whispering: 'I'm your friend, you hear me, your friend . . .' And in the mirror over the bed Luc watches Andrew bend over him and nibble at his navel. A fringe of frizzy hair tickles his stomach. The black hands take a grip on his thighs. Andrew is still wearing his trousers and tee-shirt. He is breathing heavily, and then more and more noisily. 'It's what you wanted, eh? This is what you were looking for? Tell me it's what you were looking for. Here, you see!' Andrew gets up and opens the doors of the wardrobes on either side of the bed. In each of them a strip of neon lights up: what a collection, an untidy array of whips, plastic gadgets and studded corsets. 'Which would you like? Tell me what you want.' 'But . . .' 'Come on, you know damn well what you want.' Luc shuts his eyes. Andrew leaps up, straddling him and pinches Luc's cheeks between the thumb and forefinger of both hands. 'Come on, talk, you can choose, open your eyes and look!' Luc tries to sit up. Andrew clobbers him with a good resounding slap. Luc falls back on the Missionary's lap. The Missionary blesses him. The wardrobe doors creak. Sound of metal, sound of leather. In the bathroom columns of insects were marching up the wall, insects like enormous ants with strange nightcaps on their heads and hairy legs, eight, ten, twelve hairy legs. An electric light bulb hung from the ceiling. Attracted by the light, the insects were making for it, avoiding the leprous patches of flaking paint, selecting the routes which they could best adhere to, though sometimes they fell with an unpleasant smack on the tiled floor. As he had stepped out of the bath, Luc had taken care not to tread on them, for they could still have been alive. Then he had told himself that 'he was inside Rasky's body' and that he'd really like to 'make a go of it with Rasky and pick up where they left off', but Andrew's arm was pushing him towards the bed. Ceremonial.

A whip, like a dog's lead. Andrew strikes his legs, then

his thighs, harder and harder, then his stomach and his chest. Luc bites his lips. He would like to cry out, but sharp as the pain is it also seems remote, so unbearable that it can in fact be borne. Who is striking whom? Yes, this pain will save Rasky. And the insects in the bathroom will be the first to witness his recovery. The trip to New York will at least have served some purpose. Rasky will return to Paris his old self again, with his smile, and his luggage full of bits and pieces and his gilded life of vacuity and his talent for farewell letters and telephone calls in the middle of the night. 'Come to me, I need you.' With his eyes wide open Luc is watching in the mirror canopied above him the black shadow bent on hurting him: 'You're white, anyone can see that, look and you can see. When I get beaten it leaves no marks behind. Aha!' The laughter of Chocolate returning home to find his village is going to be submerged. What a lot of things he has learnt from him, thanks to him! After the whip, then the chains and the corset, Luc is hardly conscious of anything. Except, above him, the finest picture he has seen in his life, a picture which would go on being finished off forever. No longer will he see that fixed, precise, unmoving image of himself, which used to bring him comfort and despair. He no longer belongs to himself. He is emerging from a cocoon of pain and distress.

Then Luc tells himself that he has missed out on everything. Every chance of courtesy or contemplation, all the great truths. There is nothing moral about his life anyway, just one long record of misconduct. He has missed everything on the way. So that was his body, that white thing with the over-large hips and the fine-boned angular shoulders, the rather weak chin and the rather slack face, a body ready to resign. Andrew makes a bound and grips him round the throat: 'What's on your mind?' Luc is suffocating, he is going to faint. Andrew loosens his hold. Luc gets his breath back. 'What were you thinking?'

158

Silence. 'Answer!' Again Andrew squeezes, more and more tightly. Luc gets the feeling that his eyes are going to swivel round and look into his brain. He tries to cry out. Andrew slackens his grip. Luc gets his breath back. 'Well, answer!' 'I . . .' 'Talk.' '. . . stop a moment.' 'I'll stop if you answer.' Silence. Andrew chucks on the floor all the sheets that encumber the bed, the pillows and the blankets, and shifting Luc round lengthwise on the smooth surface of the mattress, pulls out the straps level with his feet, his genitals and his neck. 'There, that'll stop you moving.' 'Let me go.' 'Where to?' 'Home.' 'Where's home?' 'To Rasky's.' 'Who's Rasky?' 'My friend.' 'He'll wait.' 'Let me alone . . .' 'What are you thinking about, what?' 'I was thinking about Tom, he's coming with his leather cushion. He'll protect me.' 'How do you expect him to get here? No-one knows where you are.' 'Tom and Bill are coming, I know they are.' Andrew smiles. 'Wait, we're gonna celebrate their arrival.' He stands up and goes to the left-hand wardrobe where he makes a choice among several knives. 'We're gonna play a little game, it's only a game, but I hope it's gonna scare you.' He sharpens a large kitchen knife, bends over Luc, bears down on Luc's stomach, and caresses Luc with the cutting edge of the blade. 'Don't move now, or you might get a little scratch.' Andrew puts down the knife, pulls a popper from his pocket and sticks it up Luc's nostrils. 'Come on, take a deep breath, come on, that's it, this'll help you take it easy, do you good, that's the way . . .'

159

Chapter Twenty-Seven

Rasky twists his head to gaze at his fourth wall, all dark glass, the opaque picture window which masks the real face of the city, looking westward. If the bed were to slide across the slippery floor and smash through his rampart wall, either Rasky would fly away or his fall would be abrupt, vertical, instantaneous, and before he had time to count the storeys, he would be a puddle down below, he would have his revenge on the slow death from within, and the flower from the gigolos of Vienna would be crushed forever. Rasky is smiling. Or he thinks he is: his lips can no longer obey his orders. There is no-one behind the bed to push him hard enough to shatter that screen which misleads him about night or day, blue sky or grey, and the life going on without him. Time has left him behind. He feels he is dragging along, outpaced. A few more steps and his strength will have given out. So he decides to fix his eyes on that window, and above all keep still. With his eyes skinned, stripped of eyebrows and lashes, riveted on the flat surface of that opaque wall concealing empty space, he lies in wait for a glimmer of light, a deepening shadow, a dark patch that would be lit up by the dawn. He remembers a phrase he used to like to quote, but who the devil wrote it? Something about the transparencies of Nature transforming appearances. There he goes, rambling on till the bitter end with his stylistic drivel. A little sign, just one tiny little sign. Like, for example, the dawn of a last day, a last waltz, the clink of ice-cubes through the air, a shattered glass in the light, the cry of some crazy bird piercing your head like a knife, Luc's smile when he withdraws from you after making love, distant and indifferent, yet gentle and

conspicuously present. A real unpretentious little Frenchman about whom he will have learnt nothing, or remark-
ably little! A bare inkling of the young man's fleeting
idealisms, his morbid quest for hope (when, how and of
what kind), his acute feeling for a kind of justice: a little
boy lost. Another parasite. Someone who, like him, would
go through life childishly thrilled by a subtle variation in
light, colour or sentiment; like a child capable of the worst
faux pas and the most spiteful injustice whenever the truth
was at stake. But what truth? The dawn could not be far
off now. Rasky knows, he can feel it, that Luc has not gone
home to 72nd Street. Has he returned to Paris? What is he
doing? Where is he? Between Rasky and Luc there has
always existed a close cat-like entente, which abolishes
distance and ignores separations. Luc calls for help. 'If the
day dawns, you'll be safe', murmurs Rasky. And he waits
for the night to pull the sheets from his bed, to tear that
curtain of opaque wall apart, to rise up and pass like a
shadow, to fan out and rescue Luc. 'Save my servant from
death, save him.' Rasky has moved. He is not sure now if
he is really talking or merely thinks he is. He can no
longer hear himself. With his left ear sunk in the pillow
and with haggard face he waits for the first sign of day,
which has not dawned yet. A glimmer would suffice.
    Lucy has pushed the couch onto the terrace. She felt
stifled. Rolled up in the fur rug, she waits trembling for
night to disperse, for the dark shape of Central Park to
emerge and take on the pastel colours of morning. Perhaps
Mister Jack is doing his rounds in the Park for her benefit,
Barnaby and Lammert lending a hand by following him
round with a wheelbarrow to collect the fallen leaves. Neat
alibi that. All three in the uniform of Health and Hygiene.
Lucy wants to take them by surprise, spy on them from on
high and leap down to join them. She shrugs her shoulders
and throws her head back. In the blackness of the black
sky she can tell that the clouds have fled: soon the roof

162

over the city will be a washed-out blue. But daylight is still a long way off. A damp smell rises from the Park, the smell of a dying summer, of autumn taking over, the scent of danger.

Rasky calls the nurse on duty and asks her to prop him up on his left side, facing the window. 'But that's bad for your heart!' 'Do what I ask, please.' 'Excuse me?' And the nurse bends close to his ear. 'Please.' A blurred word, a throaty sound, Rasky can scarcely move his lips. He is dribbling. The nurse wipes him and lightly turns him round, wedging pillows behind his back. Rasky's left arm is trapped by the weight of his body. 'You feel better that way?' Rasky dare not say that he will never be able to stay in this position: he wants to look at the window and catch the dawn. Open-mouthed, he waits.

A pigeon has just landed on the edge of the terrace, then a second and a third. Lucy dare not move in case she frightens them. They approach one another, meet and avoid each other, cooing, taking fright, fluttering away, then returning. It must be the lights from the *salon* that attract them. Barnaby never liked pigeons: an ill omen. Barnaby preferred quoting his pet authors. Stendhal: 'I alone know what I really might have done . . . other people at best can only see me as a might-have-been,' Lucy's mind is studded with magical maxims, 'my tragical maxims' Barnaby would call them, 'those you remember at nightfall, when you've nothing to do but contemplate the night. Then comes the dawn and thoughts like these fade away.' Renan: 'Such things get written in order to communicate to others the theory of the universe one carries in oneself.' Dead letters, dead phrases, Barnaby's cemetery, all these fake gems of which Lucy is the guardian. Wasn't it Wilde who said something like this: 'It is curious how vanity upholds the successful man and brings the failure down'? Lucy smiles. Suddenly she stands up, startles the pigeons and cries out to them not to come back.

163

Rasky has the impression that his squashed arm is about to be squeezed out through his fingers. He can hear the simmering of his heart. The beats slowly getting faster. Which of the two, the daylight or his heart, is going to be first at the post? 'Luc, answer me, where are you? I never told you to go away yesterday. I only told you . . .' Then Rasky decides not to get excited. The daylight is going to win. But the opaque wall merely reflects the room and the bed, another perambulator, but nobody wants to push it any more.

Rolled up in the fur rug, curled up on the couch, Lucy is watching for the dawn. She has switched off the lights in the *salon*. The pigeons will not return and they have taken with them Barnaby's cemetery of thoughts. This night with no Mister Jack is interminable. Lucy has fallen asleep.

Rasky's heart has stopped beating.

Chapter Twenty-Eight

'Wake up, so I can hit you.' That fourth article of yours, we've been waiting for your fourth article. And now, at the last moment, you think you can turn out a piece that shows you're a genius. Oh no! I'll have nothing to do with genius. I'll fling it back in your face. There's no sale for genius. We'd only get another pile of letters. And don't tell me that we only publish the readers' letters that suit us, complimentary ones if they're snappy enough and critical ones if they're stupid. Get on with that article. You have half an hour . . .

'Come on, baby, on your feet, there's plenty more for us to do.' On the corner of a table in the editor's office Luc is scribbling away on white sheets of paper, sweeping over them with his fountain pen. He twists the nib, tries to scratch it straight, wipes it on a piece of blotting-paper and licks it with the tip of his tongue. Then he shakes the pen and attempts to write, but nothing happens. Out of ink? But he has just filled it! So he squeezes out a blob of ink and dips the nib in it, but apart from the blob the ink fails to make a mark. He tries writing the words without ink, but one by one he digs a hole in every sheet. Hurry up. Only twenty minutes left. You ought to have a moment to think. Luc picks up a pencil, a piece of wood with no lead in it. So he takes a paper-knife, makes a nick in the forefinger of his left hand, squeezes out two drops of blood and dips the nib in that: at last it writes, makes a mark, he spreads the globule out and tries to form a word, but the word refuses to take shape . . .

'On your feet, beauty, on your feet.' Andrew undoes the straps and lifts Luc up. The editor enters the office. Ah!

there you are, you might have let us know you were back. That article, it's time! Luc holds out a sheet of paper with one spot of blood on it. Is that all? Yes, sir, that's all. So that's what New York means to you. You promised us a piece on the Presidential elections. Is this it? Yes, sir. Since when have you been calling me sir? Yes, sir . . . Come on, stop fooling around, give me the article. You're hiding it. No. Luc, what's got into you? Grasping him with both hands, the editor squares up to Luc, pinches his cheeks, tugs his hair and upbraids him. Come on, give me that article! What's your little game? We've no time to lose. Rasky is dead? What's that? Rasky is dead, there, he just died, I know, I can feel it. Who is Rasky? A friend, my friend. What are you going on about? My private life. I've got a private life too, old man, but I don't blurt it out. I keep it to myself. He slaps Luc. Wake up, good God, what's happened to you? It was a trap! What's that? I've been caught in a trap . . .

Andrew pushes Luc into the living-room and flings him on the floor. Rolled-up socks and dirty briefs. Luc's head is full of flashing colours, meteors that explode, meadows soaked in dew, too lush and too green, blue canopies torn asunder: through the port-hole of a plane he stretches out his arm and snatches at the blue cloth and the clouds. The editor keeps coming back to him, holding out the blood-stained page. What do you think I'm going to do with this then, eh? What am I going to do with this mark? You're a dead duck, Luc, a dead duck. And Luc wonders how he could ever have been the friend of such a bastard. He holds out his arms to his boss. He holds out his arms to Andrew. Andrew yanks his head back by the hair. 'Here, swallow this.' Two pills, a glass of water. 'Come on, swallow.' Luc gulps. 'Again.' The water trickles down his chin, forming bubbles at the corners of his mouth. 'Good, right, that's good.' He takes a grip on the nape of Luc's neck, forces him up and drives him back into the bedroom. 'This time,

166

we're gonna have fun, you wanna have fun?' Luc can feel a ball of fire growing in his stomach. He is dazzled by too many lights: he flies off into the infinite immensity of the palms of Andrew's black hands. The pages of the *Collected Adventures of Chocolate* are turning furiously, creating a violent wind. In a daze, Luc can neither see nor feel anything now. He makes one last effort and tries to explain to his boss that it is not his fault. He cries to Rasky for help, but on the pavement outside his school there is no-one waiting for him. Luc is sinking.

Only then does Andrew strip naked. Luc can no longer see him. An ebony totem streaming with sweat, he is rubbing his left fist and forearm all over with viscous jelly from a tube. Long minutes the ritual lasts. His forearm becomes a second member, which slowly, very slowly, twisting like a trepan, forces a passage into Luc, plunges and takes him. Luc is lying on his stomach, his face embedded in a pillow. When Andrew's forearm has been lodged in its most comfortable position, without loosening his hold Andrew pulls himself up over Luc's body and with his right hand, using all his force, he presses the face of the white boy down into the white pillow. He stays that way for several long minutes, holding his breath, waiting for the other to die. Death arrives on the scene unannounced. She was concealed in the pillow. Epitaph for a life: asphyxia.

Chapter Twenty-Nine

Lucy's left foot has been exposed: it is frozen. Day is dawning. Skating-rink sky. In the space of one night winter has taken over from autumn. This year there will be no Indian summer. The couch has turned into an iceberg. Lucy rips off the fur rug as one can rip a dressing from a wound. She gets up and hobbles about on one frozen foot. The light is pitiless, penetrating, not one single detail of the trees and pathways in the Park is able to escape it. Along Fifth Avenue trucks are dispensing the crush-barriers used for big parades. Tomorrow, Monday, is Columbus Day. The schools will march past for hours and hours with their banners, their male-voice choirs and their drum-majorettes.

Inside the apartment Lucy is sorting everything out, putting everything straight. She throws away scribbled notes, the corpses of exercise-books, letters from her friends in London surprised that she has been away so long, statements from the bank, the sort of rubbish accumulated by those winsome widows who go on and on for ever, believing themselves younger and more beautiful with every day that passes. Time back to front. Then Lucy returns the couch to its place. Broad daylight, a great big sun shining coldly over New York City. A dumb chill placidly stabbing you. Quick, shut the glass door! The terrace is deserted, and the *salon* neat and tidy, cleared of bits of paper and hamburgers, and the jig-saw puzzle which Lucy has just tipped in its entirety down the shoot: sound of the pieces raining down the vertical duct. Even the records have been arranged, each one back in its sleeve, all neatly lined up, and the ashtrays emptied, washed and gleaming, set out on the coffee table, that home for ash-trays, in front of the couch slowly recovering from its night in the open air. All that remains for Lucy to do is to put the closet in order, inspect the dresses, the suits and the coats, stroke the furs in their plastic covers, check that all the valuables are still in the jewel-box, the earrings with the earrings, the bracelets with the bracelets, Barnaby's cuff-links in the compartment on the left and Lammert's in the pigeon-hole on the right. It had been Lucy's task, her privilege, the last moment before they went out, to choose the links she would herself fix in their cuffs. That was how she hand-cuffed her men. Smile: Lucy closes the jewel-box. She is going to take a bath. She has got to be beautiful, she must be ready. On Sunday, day of death, day of emptiness, the cold is sure to kill someone, someone specially for her, and Lucy owes it to herself always to be positively pre-pared. Divinely beautiful. At her very best. Smile: Lucy locks herself in the bathroom. Sound of the catch. Who is she afraid of then?

Foam-bath, a Hawaii Bubble Bath, fifteen minutes of dreamy holidays, the whole ocean in a bath-tub. Antibes. Lammert is disappearing out to sea. 'You're going too far.' 'Don't worry, I'm still here.' Ah! Common expres-sions can sound quite grim at times, when they linger in the mind. Lucy is taking a dip with Barnaby and Lammert. Her children.

Lucy will never write again. She has thrown out all the exercise-books and hidden the pen-holders and the box of S-M nibs in the bottom of a drawer. She feels she has been invited out, challenged, she is ready for anything. This is what she had always longed for: to be a perfect little doll with no more reason to reproach herself for anything. One dream alone haunts and guides her: to join her babies. As simply and cleanly as possible. So she rubs the telephone with a rag dipped in surgical spirit. She wipes the receiver as fast as she can: while doing that, the line is engaged, and

170

just for once Mister Jack might call up during the day. After the telephone, she dusts the photograph of Barnaby (one kiss) and the photograph of Lammert (second kiss) and then gets dressed. Black stockings, grey suit, black scarf: very correct. In front of her dressing-table mirror she pulls a face, smiles, looks serious, pulls another face, smiles again, looks serious, then she sticks out her tongue and bursts out laughing. She brushes her hair. Puts a touch of red on her lips and sets off her eyes with one stroke of the pencil. Then, like a beautiful thoroughly healthy mare, she inspects her teeth. Her own genuine teeth. *Her* mouth isn't full of porcelain. All this of course an act she puts on for herself. Next she makes an inventory of the contents of her handbag: in the secret pocket she counts the hundred dollar bills. A jackpot for Mister Jack. She picks up the telephone. 'Kenneth?' 'Yes, madam.' 'Did you sleep well?' 'Yes, madam.' 'I'm hungry, Kenneth.' 'Oh, you ought to go out, madam, it's a beautiful day!' 'No, Kenneth, I'm expecting a phone call, could you order me some . . .'

Chapter Thirty

'Good-morning!' Carlos throws the door wide open. 'How goes our invalid now he's only malingering?' The moment he said it, the very moment he started on the 'now' and began to wonder *why* he was saying it, Carlos realised it was all over. It was the end of their little games of 'putting-baby-to-bed' and 'I'll-give-you-a-face-massage-if-you'll-tell-me-the-truth'. With delicate care he turns the corpse on its back. Rasky's left arm remains rigid, ossified, clamped to the body. The eyes have turned up, eyes of white porcelain. Carlos is used to death. The clinic where he has made his career is simply its antichamber, a last waiting-room. Ironical. But this time Rasky's death takes him by surprise. On the bedside table he had put down the box of Turkish Delight which the previous evening he had gone to buy specially for 'his' patient, knowing that Rasky adored them and that gradually, thanks to this addiction, he might recover enough strength to masticate and take nourishment. You push open the door and go into a friend's bedroom: death has come during the night with never a word. The Blue Arrow has come to a halt. We'll be late arriving in Southampton. What an unlooked-for opportunity to speak to one's neighbour, to crack a joke and, under the pretext of lighting a cigarette, to lightly touch his hand and tremble a little as you recall a friend at college who insisted on coming to take his shower with you. You? Carlos has just just missed a fine chance. One client the less. This evening the room will be occupied by someone else who will explore this whiteness, this severity, this cleanliness and the opacity of this wall of glass, a casket of death where nothing human can be heard or seen any more, not even the face of your visitors, who know that you are doomed. Carlos has sat down on the edge of the bed. So he will spend his life as a professional mourner of the living. All his life he will get to know those destinies alone which lightly touch on yours and only in the early stages impinge on your conscious mind. Later, routine takes over. But this time Rasky had broken the routine. The dying man had not even appeared astonished or enraptured when Carlos had shown him his penis and leaned over him so that Rasky with his fingertip could explore the Downtown forests. And Carlos had done this as a challenge to himself, to find out what bond he had with that particular old boy. Now what was the number of this room? And which floor, so I can warn the doctor. No, wait a bit. That idiotic nurse was responsible for this. Only she could have put him in that position. Yet he must have begged her to. Carlos tries to loosen Rasky's left arm, but the skin of the arm and the hip has become welded to the cloth of the pyjamas. Almost as if Rasky had stiffened into a refusal. He wanted to stay the way he was while waiting for the day to break. So that was it. Carlos walks up to the picture window, flattens both hands on the blind surface and leans forward with lowered head. The little French friend will have to be informed, unless he has already left for home. They're bound to find someone in the apartment, a few devoted friends in New York. Or else the servant, Odette, whose name Rasky used to mention, quoting Proust. Right. Carlos turns round. Maybe this is a dead man he'll have forgotten by next week. He is still challenging himself, wondering how he can have become so involved in the space of three days. The hope of a cure, a glimpse of escape for the two of them, the old gentleman and the gigolo? No, not that. The eyes, that's it. The eyes, the way they looked, affirming a refusal to depart, a reluctance to leave anything or anyone behind, a determination to buy up the whole earth and relieve it of all its

174

fevers. And find his recompense at the wash-house of childhood and the fountain of adolescence. Every labour merits its reward. The old man was nothing but a spoilt child. And Carlos had hunted round several shops before he had found Turkish Delight from Istanbul, genuine Turkish Delight, none of your jelly-babies, but Turkish Delight that melts in the mouth and leaves a lingering taste of sugar. Pistachio. A nice decadent taste, a decadence that is honest and authentic, nauseated by grand theories, evolutionary doctrines or the pseudo avant-garde. Rasky's naïveties were unlike anyone else's, Rasky was not like anyone. The look in his eyes in this sense was unique. Appealing. And Carlos had been only too ready to fall into the trap sprung for him by a gentleman who had had enough of female nurses. 'Death is a transvestite,' he had said to Carlos the very first day. 'It probably seems crazy to you, but I don't want any of those nurses, any of those painted-up creatures in here. They're cold. Unbending. Each time they close the door, I get the feeling they're closing the lid of my coffin. With a click, you know what I mean?' Now Rasky is filling an enormous space on the bed, he is getting bigger, his arms reaching out along the corridors of the clinic, his legs extending down the elevator shafts, choking the hospital. Carlos rubs his eyes. He would like to wipe away a tear. Not even that. On the white dial of the white telephone he composes a three-figure number. 'Doctor, can you come at once to Room . . . I'm not quite sure of the number.' Carlos lays the receiver down on the bedside-table and bumps into the chair as he crosses to the door. This time he is crying. He has gooseflesh. At his age.

Chapter Thirty-One

Andrew is sitting in the living-room, facing the portrait of Louis XIV and the portraits of himself, a mosaic of photographs pinned to the flanks of the Sun King's mount. He is pleased. Everything has gone off well. At last the moment has come for him to take his pleasure from the night's work. The risen sun is stealing through the windows, flooding across the floor, arousing the soft folds of the cast-off briefs and making the stifling atmosphere of the room unbearable. Stretched out naked, hands clasped over his penis, Andrew is contemplating Luc, the body of Luc, through the half-open door of the bedroom; the play of the light, the reflections repeated a thousand times in the mirrors lining the wardrobe doors, tossing backwards and forwards like a ball the image of the flagellated body covered in welts and in places bleeding. 'Nice work, that.' Andrew gives a deep-throated chuckle. He can see himself again as a child, kicking all day long at the empty ash-cans in that street of his in Brooklyn: he wanted to know what noise it would make, that hollow bin, that filthy cavity, and from each ash-can he drew a different sound, a different story. And then one day he decided that the city was nothing but one huge ash-can and that he could kick it like that, just for fun, to find out what noise it made. And every day the city would make a new sound. And sometimes in the ash-cans he would discover nameless wonders, anonymous victims. Oh, it wasn't *he* who attracted them: *they* came to *him*. Blind or blindfold, arms and hands bound by God knows what pressing need, what hopeful spirit of curiosity. A little guy. This one was a little guy. Luck, his name was Luck. The wretched rain was drumming insistently on the roof of the truck and the others very nearly stole Luck away from him; from *him*, Andrew, a florist's assistant by day, a specialist in cut flowers by night. That white body, his piece of candy! The flower Andrew takes in both hands this morning has not been cut. He caresses it. He strokes it. And when the sun starts to stroke the sofa on which he is lying, then Andrew will come. Whee! One fine Sunday morning. Go on then, baby, you're my beautiful baby. Now it's your turn to play. Show me what you can do. Brava, bravo! You see the little guy over there, look, have a good look, you wanted him, didn't you? Gets you all worked up, doesn't it? Attaboy, go right ahead! Sit up and beg, that's it! Brava, bravo! Whee! Andrew comes, just as the sun starts licking at the sofa. Andrew stands up, goes into the bedroom, pulls the pillow from under Luc's face and wipes his stomach with it. Then he lies down close to Luc, grabs the telephone on the far side of the bed and dials a seven-figure number. It rings. He's bound to be there, it's Sunday morning. It rings. '. . . Jack? Andrew here, I've got someone for you.' Silence. 'Yeah, at my place.' Silence. 'Yeah, right away.'

Chapter Thirty-Two

'To be frank with you, your employer died rather sooner than we expected. He had signed us a cheque for quite a substantial sum to cover care and treatment for what he thought would be a couple of months. He was sure he was going to recover. But he was a hopeless case. Quite hopeless. You knew that, didn't you?' Odette tightens her grip on the clasp of her crocodile handbag, a Christmas gift from Rasky. 'But it's too beautiful, Monsieur Rasky, it's too beautiful, I'll never dare use it.' 'Well, you did know, didn't you?' Odette shakes her head. 'Are your employer's parents still alive?' 'They died a long time ago, twenty years, I think.' 'Brothers or sisters?' 'He was an only child.' 'Cousins?' 'He never told me of any.' 'And the young man who's been visiting him lately?' 'He was Monsieur's friend. I've just come from the apartment. He wasn't there. He may have gone away for the weekend, he's left his things behind.' 'Where exactly was your employer domiciled?' 'He lived in London, Paris and here. I think he had a Portuguese passport. But he has no family left over there.' 'Has he ever spoken to you about the terms of his will?' 'Monsieur always used to say I'm not making a will and I'd simply love to see what happens when I'm dead. I thought he was joking. Monsieur used to enjoy teasing me.' 'Did your employer have a lawyer?' 'I don't know, but you could find out from Marie and Christian. In London. They work for him in London. But it's Sunday. And they have their Sundays off.' 'Did your employer see any friends in New York?' 'Just lately he never saw anyone. I used to prepare his breakfast. He would have toast, without jam. During the day he'd eat a little fruit. In the

179

evening he'd go out for a walk. Monsieur was very discreet. He was obliged to use the stairs, he was afraid of the elevator. He had slowed down so much that the gate would close on him before he could get inside and he didn't have the strength to hold it back.' 'So it's up to you to take the decisions. You want to see him?' 'See him?'

Suddenly the Doctor treats Odette with consideration, holding out his arm, opening doors for her, showing her the way, smiling politely at her. Odette does not like the role allotted to her. 'We'll have to get in touch,' she murmurs, 'with a special sort of organisation. Monsieur will have to be cremated. Monsieur had no religion.' 'Very well. We're equipped for all that here, only you will have to sign the papers.' 'Sign?' Silence. 'Perhaps we could call up the apartment after all, just to see if Monsieur Luc has come back.' 'We'll do that.' 'Or else we could try calling London, perhaps Marie and Christian haven't gone away this weekend.' 'We'll do that.' 'You know, it's the first time I've been in a situation like this.' 'I'm sure it is.'

A white room, empty benches, and on a trolley-bed Rasky's body covered by a sheet. 'You know, Doctor, I don't want to see him.' 'What have you decided, then?' Odette's hands are ice-cold. She thinks it may be the metal clasp of the handbag that is freezing her hands, or the sheer luxury of it. She is sitting very upright, her handbag hanging from a limp arm below the lower edge of her coat. It is far too big, that handbag. And inside nothing but the key to her flat, tokens for the subway and that fresh smell of new leather which Odette finds somewhat ridiculous. So Odette feels that *she* looks ridiculous. A secretary comes in with a file under her arm. Odette is invited to sit down next to the trolley-bed. Odette never used to sit down in front of Monsieur. Never. So she perches on the edge of the chair. She has her eyes glued on the bed, the sheet, that rounded shapeless form with the angular distortion lower down, like a hand held out to her. 'Here, this is where you

180

sign.' Muttered voices behind her. 'Go and find some witnesses.' 'Who?' 'Anyone, but quickly. Madam doesn't want to wait around.' They are calling her Madam now. And holding out a fountain pen. She makes an effort to sign her name clearly. Odette Blackwell, Odette Blackwell, Odette Blackwell, and as fast as she signs, the more papers she is given to sign. So the file must have been prepared a long time ago, perhaps it was made ready when Monsieur Rasky was first admitted. After every signature the secretary murmurs 'thank you, Madam.' Why thank you? When all the papers have been signed, two witnesses arrive, two nurses with purple lips and little hats on top of their heads, little white caps like paper boats. A male nurse is pushing the trolley-bed down a corridor. Cortege. Into a very wide, very noisy elevator. And down. First room to the right in the basement. The sheet covering Rasky is drawn back. Odette shuts her eyes. 'Please, Madam, we are very sorry, but you must look.' Rasky's body is placed on a conveyor. A button is pressed and the conveyor carries Rasky's body into an oven that closes behind it. Odette drops her handbag. The secretary picks it up and hangs onto it. The nurses are standing impassively on Odette's left. A strange silence settles over them. Odette is wondering if she really had the right to sign. Oh God! My God! Odette feels remote. Clasps her hands. She can no longer feel her fingers. Thinks she is about to topple forward. Recovers, by throwing her weight on both feet. 'It's nothing,' says the Doctor, 'we know it's painful for you, but it will only last a few more minutes.' In the Doctor's voice there is something commonplace which Odette finds displeasing. The minutes pass. The secretary speaks to the Doctor, a nurse clears her throat and the electrical vibrations from the oven cease. Odette watches the gate open again and the conveyor returns. The male nurse who had been pushing the bed now sweeps the ashes from the conveyor and puts them in a white plastic cube-shaped box.

181

He passes the box to the Doctor, who hands it to Odette. The secretary opens Odette's handbag: the box just fits inside. More papers to sign, the nurse first, then the Doctor, then the secretary, then Odette. 'This time,' says the Doctor, 'it is all over.'

In the entrance hall to Sutton Hospital Carlos stands waiting, with one small suitcase. The Doctor motions to him to hand it over to Odette. 'All Monsieur Rasky's personal effects are inside, would you like to check them?' Odette shakes her head. Any moment now she is going to start sobbing stupidly. And she does not want to sob stupidly in front of everyone. It is all too much for her. And it is not part of her job. 'Would you like us to call you a taxi?' Odette shakes her head. She will take the subway, with the box of Turkish Delight in the suitcase and Rasky in her handbag.

Chapter Thirty-Three

D'Averiano Laundry, 24-hour cleaning, delivery service. Mister Jack inspects himself in the rearvision mirror: Lucio's delivery-man's uniform doesn't suit him too badly, especially the cap, and it's fun driving a laundry van, it smells good and never goes above forty. A white funeral. 'What you gonna do with my vehicle and my clothes?' 'It's no business of yours, Lucio, I wanna play a trick on a girl I gotta date with, a good lay.' 'Oh Jack, you'll never change.' 'Why should I? It's a deal worth five hundred bucks.'

'That was fast work!' 'At your service, sir.' Sarcastic smile from Mister Jack. 'Come on in!' Andrew is pulling on his pants. 'Don't bother to get dressed, bud, I'll make delivery on my own. I'm a big boy now. It's better you don't go out.' Silence. Mister Jack throws two large grey sacks on the sofa and strokes his moustache. 'Besides, it's the first time I've seen you in the nude. Not bad, from behind you look like a real black broad. Pity I'm not your side of the fence.' 'In here!' Andrew points to the bedroom. Mister Jack pokes his head round the door. 'Phew! Not bad. Only gotta clean him up a bit. You knew him?' 'No.' 'Sure?' 'Sure, promise.' 'Nobody see you together?' 'Yeah, but only folk who don't talk.' 'Who then, tell me who, so I know if you're doing me a favour, like you did before, or whether this one's gonna get me busted.' 'The truck guys.' 'Well, that's O.K., beauty, O.K.' Mister Jack appears to be thinking. 'Come on, take your pants off and let me have a peek at what goes on there. It's giving me ideas. I wanna try it.' Silence. 'And then you gotta be nice to me, ain't you? With all that fine laundry I'm taking away, and no charge either.' 'Maybe you'd like me to pay you. I know damn well what you're gonna do with Luc.' 'That the guy's name?' 'Forget it.' Mister Jack sticks his hands into the pocket of Lucio's overalls. Holes in the pockets of that son of a bitch, Lucio doesn't waste his time either. 'Well, what about those pants, that's it . . . Bravo . . . Turn around, oh Jeez, walk around the sofa . . . lie down . . . what you do to that guy, eh? Tell.' Andrew stretches out, hands clasped behind his neck, and stares up at the ceiling. 'Play the Queen of Sheba, would you? Don't blame me if I want my pay-off. Look, look at me. Does this interest you? Oh beauty! Did you have a ball last night! Lift your legs up and spread 'em. That's right. A bit more. Perfect.' Mister Jack slips his shoes off without taking his hands from his pockets, then he goes up to the sofa and kneels down facing Andrew. 'Well, this turn you on? You get the feeling that guy over there is watching us. Does that bug you? Not me. Let's get on with it. Oh!' Mister Jack has pulled a button off, opening his flies. Good thing, too, Lucio will imagine his date went off fine. Andrew is all black on the outside, all hot within. 'Christ! You're a real little Queen. Played at being top man yesterday, did you? But you sure seem to be enjoying this!' Andrew looks round the bedroom, at the sliding door, the bed, Luc's body, the wardrobe doors with their mirrors and the objects hanging in the wardrobe, all those fetishistic gadgets. 'How'd you do away with this one, with a pillow like last time, eh? Come on, beauty, tell me, eh, or I'll split you in two.' Andrew braces himself, shuts his eyes. Mister Jack's hands clasp him round the hips. Mister Jack holds still. He grunts. Grimaces. Andrew can no longer understand what Mister Jack is saying. 'Phew, we must do this again, beauty, O.K.' Silence. 'O.K.?' Mister Jack stands up, picks up his fly button, then chucks it away: it will look better not to take it with him, in a case like this buttons usually get lost. 'Right, to work!'

In the sack from the D'Averiano Laundry there are ropes and other sacks. 'We'll truss him up like a joint of meat, O.K.? Lend me a hand.' Mister Jack takes hold of Luc by the feet. Andrew by the shoulders. 'We'll wash him here, if that's O.K. by you.' They lay Luc in the bath-tub. 'Say, do you have strangers in your bathroom! There are products, you know, that get rid of these creepy-crawlies.' Silence. Mister Jack turns on the shower. 'Unless you like that kinda thing.' 'What's that?' Mister Jack shouts: 'Unless you like that kinda thing, beauty.' 'Quit calling me beauty, will you?' 'What do you want me to call you, Shanghai Lily? Get scrubbing.' Luc's open mouth fills with water. Mister Jack tries to close it, impossible: the mouth is set firm, as if locked. 'Say, Lily, you must have gone a bit wild, you sure he didn't catch on?' Mister Jack smashes his fist into the jaw. It closes. 'It's better that way, or he'd be bloated, the bastard.' They turn Luc over and scrub the lacerated back. 'How long did it go on, Lily's little party?' No reply. Andrew shuts off the water. Mister Jack is staring at Luc's body, at the mouth near the plug-hole and the drowned insects spinning round. 'Hope those little sneaks don't tell tales out of school. Right, you dry while I hold him.' 'No towels.' 'Go fetch your pants.'

Luc's body on the floor, by the fireplace. 'He didn't by any chance leave you his return ticket to Paris? I was just feeling like a little trip over there.' Silence. Slowly Mister Jack bends Luc's legs at the knees and folds the arms round the legs. 'I have to move fast or his legs will be stiff as pokers.' Mister Jack ties Luc up. Andrew puts his finger on the knots. 'Got some scissors? That's it . . . I'll cut it, gotta save it. Oh, take this . . .' Mister Jack has sliced off a lock of hair and offers it to Andrew. 'Souvenir, I guess you dig souvenirs.'

Andrew and Mister Jack put Luc's trussed-up body in a sack, then this first sack into a larger sack, and then into another still larger one. D'Averiano Laundry, 24-hour

185

cleaning, delivery service. Mister Jack is standing by the bundle, stroking his moustache. 'When do you want all this back, Lily beauty?' Andrew shrugs his shoulders, moves to the door and opens it. No-one on the staircase. He signs to Mister Jack that he can go. Mister Jack lifts his load over his shoulder. 'Gee, ma'am, but your dirty linen weighs heavy.' He passes in front of Andrew. 'Turn around one last time and show me the world's end!' Laugh. Andrew slams the door, goes straight into the bathroom, drops the lock of hair into the toilet and flushes it down. Tomorrow he will go and see the Columbus Day Parade, like everyone else.

Chapter Thirty-Four

Odette sets the cube of white plastic down on the desk, next to the typewriter. Why, Monsieur Luc has been writing something: 'My pockets are full of a crazy collection of marbles. I count them again and again and I always have the same number. I play against myself, win or lose, my pockets bulge with glass marbles and alley taws. I count them again and again and I always have the same number. No score. Match drawn. Time passes and leaves me as it found me. It takes nothing, gives nothing, and I languish. I have no existence. Before Rasky, like a bit-part player, leaves me, walks off my stage and out of my theatre and my show, shall I discover the keyword that will break me down and make a hole in my pocket full of marbles, and yet still hand me over all complete to someone, just once, at least once in my life? It's the finest present I could give him. The finest present I could give myself. Not a hope . . .' Odette pushes the typewriter to one side. Moves the plastic cube right opposite the armchair. That is the best place for it, isn't it? She is not quite sure. As she turns away, her foot catches in the carpet; she nearly trips but steadies herself by clutching at the edge of a chest of drawers. This house is driving her away. The cube is watching her. She is afraid. But what if she were to wait for Monsieur Luc? Or put a call through to London? 'Opeator, will you get me BAL 8291. That's right, 91, London.' Flowers wilting in the vase next to the telephone: Monsieur Luc forgot to change the water. Bed unmade in the bedroom: Monsieur Luc forgot to make his bed. 'No answer? It's a large house, will you let it ring a few moments?' White cube in the middle of the table. The ashtrays are full of cigarette ends. Monsieur Luc has scribbled a telephone number on the memo-pad: illegible. 'No answer. Thanks. Thank you.' Odette hangs up. The postman has slipped some letters under the door. They are for Monsieur Rasky. Odette stacks them up in a pile on the desk by the cube. Then she opens the suitcase. The Portuguese passport, the address books, the leather folder containing Luc's last letters and his telegram 'Arrive tomorrow Air France Flight 913. Love Luc.' Then there is a wallet for credit cards, an alarm-clock, a watch, a silver triptych with three photos, Rumanian father, Portuguese mother and in the middle Luc in bathing trunks at Capri, Easter 1968. Odette lays them all out round the white cube. Blue silk pyjamas, dressing gown to match, pigskin slippers and a box of Turkish Delight. Odette stares at the white cube. 'Please may I take the Turkish Delight, Monsieur Rasky?' Silence. 'Thanks, Monsieur Rasky, thank you.' Then, standing in front of the desk, holding the box like a little girl who has just been given first prize for good conduct, she murmurs in a quavering voice: 'What am I going to do now? Tell me what I ought to do.' Wait? Wait for Monsieur Luc? Send a telegram to London? And what if I had no right to sign those papers? What if Sutton Hospital had made a mistake and took advantage of me to . . .? Odette removes her coat, puts on her apron for work and opens all the windows. Draughts, a flurry of sunshine and wind, the acacia-tree in the courtyard at the back of the building is quite tousled. And the wind is tormenting it. Odette will do the housework: and meanwhile thinks of nothing. Perhaps Monsieur Luc will come back. She disposes of the dirty sheets and replaces them with nice clean pink ones. She shakes the blankets out the window, then the bedcover and the two pillows, and she tucks the bed in squarely, impeccably. Then she unpacks Monsieur Luc's suitcase, hangs up the trousers and shirts, a dinner-jacket, a blue suit and four ties. She clears two drawers in Monsieur Rasky's dressing-table and fills them with Monsieur Luc's briefs, socks and tee-shirts. And with every movement she makes she is striving to forget her signature, her journey back in the subway (people looked at her very oddly, at least that was her impression, unless . . .), the white plastic cube around which she tries to arrange things in some sort of order as a prelude to her own fears, as if something inside her was about to crack. Then, as a consolation, she opens the box of sweetmeats and bites into her first Turkish Delight. She closes her eyes: it melts in her mouth, it is sugary, almost sickly, but the excessive sweetness delights and calms her. Then in the centre she crunches a pistachio nut, bitter-sweet, a delicate taste at first, then a sharpness that cleaves the throat like a blade. So *that* was Turkish Delight, Monsieur's favourite treat, one layer of sweetness and another that veers to the aggressive. In the kitchen Odette pours herself a glass of water and tries with a drink to chase the taste away, but it is no good, the taste is engrained. Monsieur Rasky would always take a siesta after his coffee, after his Turkish delight. He liked to go to sleep no doubt with that taste in his mouth.

Vacuum cleaner, electric polisher, a flick with the duster round the picture frame, Odette even dusts the lampshades, she empties the wastepaper baskets, washes out a pile of ashtrays, sprays through the whole apartment with deodorant, changes the light-bulb in the lamp next to the telephone, sharpens the pencil for the memo-pad, throws out the withered flowers and cleans the putrid-smelling vase once, twice, three times, scouring the inside to dispel the unpleasant odour of dead flowers that have been standing too long. In the bathroom she clears the little cupboards, cleans the glass shelves with spirit, scrubs the wash basins, disinfects the toilet bowl, washes the shower-curtain and goes hunting for the last of the scurvius: armed with insecticide, she kneels on the floor, spies out

189

the entrances to their hidden lairs all round the bath tub, and empties the aerosol bomb. She has tied a towel round her face as a protective mask. Her eyes are smarting. She shuts the bathroom door behind her, telling herself that 'there can't be a single one of those horrid creatures still alive, inside or behind the tiles!' And by the time the apartment is thoroughly spruce, with the cube of white plastic enthroned on a scintillating desk, the wall-clock is gravely striking five. She calls up London: still nobody. And Monsieur Luc has not come back. So then she folds up her apron and, smoothing it with her hands, puts it neatly in the suitcase from the hospital. Then she lays on top of it her rubber gloves, her working slippers and two dust cloths that belong to her, not forgetting the box of Turkish Delight. She puts her coat on. Lays hands for the last time on the cube of white plastic, says farewell to Monsieur Rasky and leaves. Odette has done all she had to do. First thing tomorrow, she will telegraph London, and then they will do what *they* have to do.

Chapter Thirty-Five

Carlos under the shower. He turns up the hot water: a stinging hot shower. Then he switches to cold water: a violent cold shower. He plays about, standing directly under the jet so that the water bounces strongly off the top of his skull, splashing all over the white mosaic walls and the glazed door. A new day, a new patient. Next week-end he will go down to Southampton and his Mom will find that he looks a bit sad, a bit dejected. She will ask him questions. He will shrug his shoulders. But in the train back maybe he will exchange a few words with someone, swap telephone numbers and break the spell cast by his idea for a film. He will become part of his own film and he will play the star role. Basta. Carlos crouches under the shower, soap in hand. He soaps round his toes, the soles of his feet, the heels, rubbing vigorously, working up a lather. Then he comes up to the calf, the front and the back, and behind the knees, massaging himself so he gets the feeling he is scouring himself clean. Then the thighs, a manikin of foam with foamy pants: he straightens up and rinses himself down. Picks the soap up again and washes his neck, rubs all over his face, head and hair, with his eyes shut very tight: rinses. Round his chest, nipples like press-studs, brown, very brown, armpits, hips, stomach, down to the navel: rinses. A long long rinse. He opens his eyes again and this time soaps his genitals, his buttocks, his crotch. A strange feeling comes over him, the soap works like magic, frothing up, neatly gripped in the palm of his left hand, moving in constant circles, caressing his skin and his body-hair. The soap massages and bubbles in tune with the water, there is magic in the soap! Rasky is in the soap!

191

Idiot. Rasky is in the soap! Stop, Carlos, stop it! Rasky is in the soap. He massages, cleanses and purifies. Pure, what does the word pure mean? Rasky has grown quite small, quite sorry for himself, quite soft. Rasky has won the game. Impossible. Carlos rinses down, kisses the soap and lays it in the soap-tray. There is a trace of bitterness on his lips. He runs his tongue over them. Then rinses his mouth and spits, rinses and spits again.

Floor 27, Room 2713, Carlos pushes the door open. 'Good morning, sir, my name is Carlos, your new nurse. The Doctor has sent me . . .'

Chapter Thirty-Six

'This time I'm gonna have fun.' Mister Jack rubs his hands together. 'Every day is not a Sunday.' Mister Jack is in his shirtsleeves. 'The old bag's gonna get her money's worth.' He sets Luc down, unties him and lays him out before he gets too stiff. Then he has an idea: he sits Luc down on a chair for a while. He has plenty of time. He leaves Luc all alone, closes and triple-locks the door of the Chapel, then sets off for Lucio's, invites him to lunch and tells him all about his high jinks. 'She was black as your hands when you're tinkering with the engine of your van, and I paid a little visit through the back door, to see what it was like when she kissed me with her real mouth.' Lucio punctuated his friend Jack's narrative with an admiring 'Hey, man!' or 'Wowww!' 'Say, there's no bottom to your pockets, they're all holes, you never said you always kept your hand on the starter, ready to shoot off at any time.' Lucio explodes into laughter and clinks glasses with Mister Jack. Then Mister Jack returns to the Chapel about five p.m. He switches the telephone over to the Answering Service, takes off his jacket and rolls up his sleeves; he moves the davenport out of his office, a decrepit old piece he has no more use for, together with the low table that goes with it. He will soon have enough bread to buy his own business, so he can quite well promise himself a nice little desk, brand new, with designer armchairs, so that his clients have to pay through the nose and feel all the better for it. His real clients, those with a corpse to dispose of. And the others on his waiting list, those in purgatory, who worship the dead.

Mister Jack puts the davenport up on the podium, with

the table in front of it. Then in one corner of the couch, he sets Luc down, the left arm leaning on the black satin armrest and the right hand lying on the right knee. Between the middle finger and the forefinger he inserts a True cigarette (filter cigarettes, latest United States Government test, twelve mgs. tar, 0.7 mgs. nicotine, the anti-cancer cigarette). Then he sees that Luc's feet are planted flat on the floor, drapes the penis, combs the hair and opens the eyes wide. A stroke of the pencil restores their look of animation. A touch of powder and he masks the traces of violence on the cheeks, the pinch-marks and the scratches. 'Jeez! Black Lily must have had a ball!' All that was missing from the scene was an ice-bucket on the low table, with two glasses, a bottle of soda and a flask of whisky. Not forgetting the packet of Trues and the book of matches: Luc is waiting for someone to light his cigarette. A naked young man on a couch is expecting a lady visitor. A picture drawn straight from life, which at times is a stagnant pool whose surface nothing can ruffle, not even the winds of some freakish storm or the stones thrown by village children from the edge, stones subsiding through the water as though it were mud, with never a splash or an eddy, an immaculate job, the dismal lament of a drowned man soundlessly immersed. Mister Jack is pleased with himself. It's a surprising setting, which is bound to delight his client from Lusaka, the lady from London who is filthy rich, always so nice and respectful with his corpses. A really grand client.

Spying through the see-through mirror in his office, Mister Jack is adjusting the lighting effects. A little blue here, a little pink there, and artificial daylight on the couch to make it all more realistic. Music: he twiddles the knobs on the control panel, a little organ music in stereo. Great. What a show! Everything is ready.

Leaving all the lights on, he walks out of the Chapel and goes two or three blocks up West End Avenue to the corner of 87th Street, where he enters a snack bar and orders a double hamburger, rare, with onions, french fries and a black coffee. 'Where's the telephone?' He looks at his watch: half past six on a Sunday evening, with the sun setting over Central Park. It's worth five hundred bucks, this job. And why not six hundred? Make it six hundred. 'Hello, this is Mister Jack.' Silence. 'Can I speak to Madam Lucy?' 'Yes, yes.' A thin trembling voice. Make it seven hundred. 'I have a present for you.' 'When?' 'Right away.' 'All for me, on my own?' 'Just for you!' 'Where?' 'I'll wait for you at the snack-bar on the corner of 87th and Columbus Avenue. Come on foot.' Silence. 'You don't ask me how much?' 'No. I'm coming.' 'I'll wait.' Click. Mister Jack hangs up. Settle for eight hundred, serve her right, for not asking how much.

Chapter Thirty-Seven

'I'll look prettier in the green dress, that's it, the green dress, quick, Lucy, quick, Mister Jack's waiting for you.' Lucy takes a deep breath, pulls up the zipper at the back, gives a few little flicks to the folds of the skirt to loosen them out, tries out an emerald pendant to mask her neck a little and then opts for a pearl necklace, all very plain and quite cold after lying so long in the jewel box: a gift from Lammert. 'Quick!' A touch of powder on the tip of her nose, a dab of perfume behind the ears, two strokes of transparent lipstick and a suspicion of blue on the eyelids. 'Clashes with the dress, but what the hell . . .' Grey coat, black scarf: Lucy checks in her handbag to make sure she has forgotten nothing, money, a thousand dollars. 'One never knows, if I'm really going to be all alone.' Lucy leaves all the lights on. She will feel less frightened when she comes home.

'A cab, Madam?' 'No, thank you, Kenneth, I'm going to walk.' 'It's cold outside, Madam!' 'I'll walk fast.' 'See you later, Madam, have a good evening. 'See you later, Kenneth.' Lucy passes in front of the Park Lane and the Navarro, then she cuts across by the Lincoln Center and walks up Columbus Avenue, counting the streets, counting her paces. Various men make straight for her. Lucy evades them, concealing her handbag under her coat and burying her face in the black scarf. Darkness is falling. An icy wind gets up. 71st Street. She is afraid of being late. Going past the Philharmonic Hall she remembers that Bach concert. The *Magnificat* was on the programme. Lucy had gone there with Barnaby, and as usual Barnaby had the score on his lap. He adored that: with his spectacles on the end of his nose, he would read the music from the open book. And Lucy had never liked the sound of Barnaby's right hand sliding up the next page, turning up the corner and playing with it with his finger when the concert was not up to standard, then turning the page and so on. And Lucy would rejoice in the Shsh's and the Be Quiet's of their neighbours disturbed by the rustle of the pages. She could not stand it either, but dared not say so. 'But I'm not making any more noise than they do, continually fiddling with their programmes,' Barnaby would claim, 'or unfolding the paper wrappers round their candy. So far as I know, there's no law against following a score.' Lucy would not answer. She would just smile, rest her hand on Barnaby's hand and cast him a tender look. But that day, during the *Magnificat*, she had wondered why Barnaby's love and attention were so dependent upon signs, when this magical anthem in celebration of the world was soaring above the flat surface of the pages of the score. Something that was merely written down in black and white, in a prison of signs and lines, was for the brief moment of that concert flooding a whole area of space, with chorus, soloists and orchestra and the conductor's baton to set the time and pace. So between Lucy and Barnaby there existed this mild divorce. Lucy would give herself utterly to the anthems of the earth while Barnaby was still absorbed in their alchemy. And that was the way it had been with everything. This evening, Lucy is thinking that a sidewalk is simply the score of a rhapsody for a city. New York City on the eve of Columbus Day, with no Indian Summer and the first daggers of winter: a corpse is simply the musical score of a life . . . and now here she is too, getting absorbed in signs, the materiality of writing. *Magnificat*: was Barnaby seeking to decipher something else? Perhaps he was amazed at what can arise from the surface of a text; perhaps in those marks and shapes and patterns, that algebra of notes and keys, he was trying to catch the secret of creation, a man whose reputation consisted solely of being a distinguished analyst, a professor of political economy, influential, successful and dilettante, who had been able to dispense with a career in the Diplomatic Service in order to indulge in the luxury of being a teacher and critic. Perhaps Barnaby was seeking what in general terms is called life, all those things that revolve round a clearly defined form, that undefinable world of sensations and feelings and emotions evoked by a text which has the impoverished look of the written, the printed word. Pages, nothing but pages.

And hadn't Lammert asked Lucy one day to read out loud the scene of Richard II's farewell, while he followed the text? Lucy's voice had trembled a little. Lammert had confessed to her with a laugh: 'you'd make a pretty awful tragic actress.'

86th Street. Lucy sees the sign outside the snack-bar. She feels reassured. She has arrived. She hears the beating of her heart. That too sets the pace. She is anxious to see the partner for her date.

Chapter Thirty-Eight

The theme song of New York is anonymity, perfect anonymity. It wraps around you, covers you up and sets you longing for the hypocritical lays of the cities of Old Europe, the pathetic dirges of cities where famine stalks and the exotic chanting of cities where the samba or the sirtaki reigns supreme. The song of New York City is wondrous in its anonymity. But the wonder turns rapidly to boredom: the end of the line. The rule is all or nothing and nobody any the wiser. It is either too hot or too cold, either it rains cats and dogs or the sky is too blue, the air too keen or the sun too bold, everything is either too scruffy or too stunning. And each of them in one small corner, all its citizens are taking stock, sorting themselves out. Everyone becomes his own assassin. And the anonymous snares are crammed with victims. *Fin de siècle.*

In the restroom of the snack-bar Lucy is rolling up a little bundle of bank notes: nine hundred dollars, expensive, but if she can stay the whole night and be there all alone . . . pooh, it's only paper. Besides, Lucy tells herself, she spends nothing during the day and the Veronese Suite has been rented for another thirteen months. How do you envisage your future? I don't. Lucy counts the bills again. She still has several hundred dollars left to hire a cab at dawn, more than she needs, futile to count, she shrugs her shoulders, smiles and, clutching the roll of bank notes in her left hand and for form's sake working the flush with the right, she walks out with dignity. 'Here you are.' Mister Jack pockets the money. 'Let's go!'

Lucy finds it hard to keep up with Mister Jack. When she adapts her pace to the pace of the Brylcreemed dancer, he changes the rhythm, pretends to miss a beat and shunts from left to right, from right to left: he doesn't want her walking idiotically beside him. So Lucy walks behind Mister Jack. They are about to enter the Chapel by the side gate, through a yard stinking of ashcans and mouldering garbage. When the door has closed behind her, Lucy will breathe a sigh of relief. Mister Jack secures all the locks. 'There we are, now it's all yours, through there, you know the way.' Silence. 'I'm going to watch T.V. in my office. When you want to leave or if there's anything at all you need, there's a bell on the left of the podium marked Office. Push the button and I'll come down.' 'Thanks.' 'Don't thank me, take your time. See you later.'

Four at a time Mister Jack mounts the stairs that lead to his office and slams the door. Lucy is alone, alone at last, she feels at home in her own little realm. She pushes the leather door which opens directly onto the podium. Organ music, soft lights. 'He' is waiting for her, sitting on a couch. 'He' is white. 'He' is fair. First of all Lucy sees his shoulders, the back of his neck. A sigh: the leather door closes by itself. Lucy undoes her scarf and her coat, puts her handbag down on a chair, folds the coat and the scarf, clasps her hands as if she were about to pray and stands there stiffly for minutes on end, breathing in the stuffy air and the mingled odour of old leather, incense and dust. Lucy has never seen a corpse before that wasn't laid out flat. And this one is seated. Lucy has never been alone with a corpse before. And this one is waiting just for her. This is the happiest day of her life. She walks up to the couch. 'May I sit down?' She sits.

An empty room: the family in the front row, the Demoiselles of Carpentras, the pupils' parents, little Jewish hair-pulling girls, cousins from Venasque and friends from Séguret, Michel and his parents, Michel who would have so much liked to have married Lucienne Roussel. An empty room: Cousin Elia is in the third row wearing her

202

dark-brown camel-hair coat, it's the fashion, with that revolting habit she has of poking her fingers up her nose when she's bored, so she must be bored now. An empty room: there is the governess of the Ambassador's children, the 'formidable lesbian', podgy in her flat-heeled shoes. She is there out of a sense of obligation, and now working in a firm that manufactures clothes for children, makes frillies for the under-tens and specialises in little girls. For the coming winter she 'predicts' that little girls will be extremely feminine, in very short coats with raglan sleeves and pleated skirts. She still writes to Lucy from time to time, and Lucy has never dared tell her to stop. An empty room: there are Barnaby's friends, the London gentry, with smooth featureless faces, as though they had all donned stocking masks to preserve their incognito, avoid all recognition. Time has eroded them, like a marble phallus. If they only knew that they could remind one of a marble phallus. 'What's a phallus, *Maman*?' asks Lucienne on a visit to the *Musée Lapidaire* at Avignon. 'A sort of butterfly, Lucienne, before it gets its wings.' What a fib. An empty room: Barnaby is sitting in the back row on the left, following the score of the *Magnificat*. He is trying to turn the pages silently, asking to be forgiven. Lucy would like him to look up. Lucy would like to see his face once again, just one more time. But Barnaby doesn't move. An empty room: there's Lammert, sitting in the back row on the right. He is reading too. The farewell of the Queen to Richard II. Reading and re-reading the same page, the forefinger of his left hand sliding along the line and then, as soon as he has reached the bottom of the page, skipping up to the top and starting all over again. Lammert is not leaning so far forward as Barnaby: Lucy catches a glimpse of his lips moving as he reads aloud, but she can hear nothing. The room is empty. Lucy is pleased: everyone is present. She bends closer to the young man. 'What is your name?' On the naked shoulder she can pick out a small tattoo-mark, very small and discreet, practically effaced, 'Luc & Rasky' in a rose with three thorns. 'Is your name Luc?' Silence. 'Is your name Rasky?' Silence. Lucy leans forward and stares fixedly at the young man's face. 'No, you're French and your name is Luc.' End of the First Act. Lucy feels sure of herself. 'I'm French too, you know. *Je viens du Midi.* You see, Luc, I can still remember that accent.' Lucy's voice strangles. She takes a deep breath. 'My name is Lucienne, but everyone calls me Lucy.' Just as she is saying 'everyone', she looks into the empty room: everyone is listening to her. She stands up. 'This is my green dress, my mascot, my good-luck charm. Do you like it, Luc?' Silence. 'Oh, don't say anything, there's no need to answer, I *know* you like it, Luc. Everyone has always liked it. It's never out of fashion. I've shortened it of course, now you can see my knees, but the bust-line hasn't changed, it's completely me. It's my style.' Silence. Organ music. Lucy twirls around. 'This dress makes me want to dance, it's almost like wearing a second skin, my second skin.' Silence. 'You don't want to dance, you don't know how? Never mind, Luc. We'll just talk, shall we?'

Mister Jack is at his desk counting the money, smoothing out the hundred dollar bills with the tips of his fingers, putting them all right side up in a neat little pile and re-counting them. Then he slips them into his wallet. Too bulky. So he puts them into an envelope, which he seals and marks: 'bills to be paid.' He giggles. He thinks what fun he is having all by himself and how good it makes him feel. Sometimes at night he dreams of something funny that makes him laugh, till his own laughter wakes him up. And makes him uneasy.

Lucy takes a True cigarette from the low table and lights it. 'Oh, I'm sorry . . .' She kneels down in front of the couch and extending her arm towards Luc's right hand holds the lighted match to the tip of his cigarette. 'You wait and see how I light it, as if nothing had happened to you and it was all going to start again for me!' She drops the match in the ashtray and blows on Luc's cigarette, a steady draught increasing in intensity: soon smoke is rising from the cigarette. 'You see!' A lovelight. 'Do you feel better? I do!' Lucy sits down again next to Luc, a little closer to Luc, occasionally leaning over to blow on Luc's cigarette and keep it burning. 'You'll smoke it right down to the end, won't you?' Occasionally too she brings the ashtray up to the cigarette wedged between Luc's fingers and gives it a gentle tap for the ash to fall in the ashtray. 'That's fine, you see, it wasn't so difficult, was it?' She crosses her legs, lies back on the couch, folds her arms and smokes her own cigarette, first closing then opening her eyes to watch the smoke rings rise. 'The smoke doesn't bother you, I hope?' Silence. 'Do you think I'm ridiculous?' Silence. 'Careful, you're going to burn yourself.' Lucy crushes out her own cigarette, takes Luc's cigarette and stubs his out in the ashtray. Luc's hand drops from his knee to the couch. Lucy screams, springs up, rushes to the side of the podium and presses the button marked 'Office', one, two, three times. She dare not turn round to look. She is frightened. Again she presses the button and leaves her finger on it. Twenty or thirty seconds: Mister Jack opens the leather door. 'He moved, Mister Jack, he moved!' Mister Jack shrugs his shoulders and retires. 'Don't go!'

Lucy crosses her arms: she has goose-flesh and her throat feels dry. She walks to the low table, drops two ice-cubes in one of the glasses and pours out a small whisky, without soda. She wants it neat. She looks at Luc and whispers: 'You know you frightened me? You know that don't you?' And she goes to the back of the room, on the left, to sit next to Barnaby.

The old bag's getting jumpy. Mister Jack switches on the television, some bawling show, tries another network, a commercial, flips about, a Western, gun shots, flips again, too noisy, but it's broadcast live, a young girl

205

telling how she left her family, how she became pregnant and had an abortion. A link-up with her parents, who tell her all is forgiven and she can come back home: interesting. Mister Jack lies flat on the floor facing the set, splits open a bag of popcorn and nibbles away like a squirrel, while he sees how the rest of the world lives. 'An ugly cow like that! How did she find a stud to lay *her*! What are they paying her to tell *her* little story? Her parents, my ass, it's all rigged!' Mister Jack watches and listens. He's enjoying it. That's what he calls life!

Lucy removes her shoes. 'They're hurting, I'm not really used to walking, and just now I had to come on foot.' She sits cross-legged in front of the couch and with the tip of one finger strokes the upper part of Luc's feet. 'What's the good of explaining everything, especially when it doesn't matter. I'm here and I want to stroke your feet. So I'm stroking them.' She flattens her hands on Luc's feet and seizes hold of them. 'You're almost as cold as I am. Tell me who hurt you. You're black and blue. Tell me, don't leave me to guess all alone.' Silence. 'You have the legs of a swimmer, you too. You could have taken me far out into the open sea. It would have been another first day, one of those days when you feel that you're making a fresh start and it's going to begin all over again. We're always dreaming of a love that's going to be better than the last one, and stupidly all we do is make an inferior imitation of the past, each time worse than the last.' Silence. 'And that's why I'm here. We're here together.' Lucy rests her head against Luc's knees. 'A young Frenchman, that was missing in my life. I never had time to really get to know any young Frenchmen. I was dreaming of somewhere else. That was the air hostess in me. Deep down inside me I was longing to spread my great big net and catch the whole earth in it, to follow the clouds drifting over Carpentras, way above my balcony, and see the whole world adrift in space. Then at times I told myself that the clouds were standing still and it was only the earth that was turning. In a way the clouds were only the watch-towers of a huge concentration camp. Then with a gust the *mistral* would call me to order and the clouds were sailing off too, in all directions at once, but they were on the move. And the earth was still going round as usual. It was Barnaby who was always saying: "Oh, if only the Earth could take us all by surprise." It's a strange story, my story about the clouds, but I know you understand it.' Silence. 'You're not smiling, not making fun of me. You're the best listener I've ever had. And I'm not mad, you know. No, no, I feel fine with you, with me talking and you listening. I'm listening to you as well.' Lucy is slowly stroking Luc's thighs. 'My mother always used to call my dolls my playmates. I could never understand why. Today I understand: you are my playmate. We'll go to the Garoupe, a little beach near Antibes, I'm sure you know it, it's not far from the fountain of the child Septentrion. You remember the epitaph? *Saltavit et placuit*, he danced and brought delight. He pleased and was loved by everyone. We all go the same way, don't we? You danced too, but who was it hurt you?' Lucy stands up. 'Do you want a whisky? One or two ice-cubes, a dash of soda, tell me what you like, you're not going to let me drink alone.' Silence. 'Right. The same as me.' Lucy fills two glasses. 'Here.' She wedges the glass between Luc's right hand and his knee. The glass tips over, falls and smashes. She mops up, and collects the fragments. 'It's lucky to break clear glass. Here, drink from mine.' She offers her glass to Luc's lips. 'Have a sip.' Her hands tremble a little. 'There.' The whisky runs down Luc's chest. 'That's fine.' Silence. 'You see, you were thirsty.' Silence. 'I knew you were thirsty, we both feel thirsty together, we think together. I'm sure the story of your life is like mine. Tell me about your tattoo. Tell me. Tell me.' Lucy caresses Luc's lips. 'We give everything and we give nothing, don't we?' With the forefinger of her right

207

hand she tries to separate Luc's lips. 'One word, just say one word, that's it, I'm right . . .' 'We have everything, and then we have nothing . . .' 'I understand you . . . Say something else, your voice is soft, something of Barnaby's, something of Lammert's, exactly as I was hoping, the voice of a friend, a frank and honest voice, when our story seems to be nothing but one gigantic lie. Yet here I am and here you are. You don't mind if I caress you, do you? Your skin is so soft.' Lucy brushes her lips over the tattoo mark. 'Luc, I started by calling you by your name, by calling you Luc. Then I was afraid, I think you made me feel shy.' Again she touches the tattoo mark with her lips, and her teeth play with the marble skin. Her lips skate over it. Lucy shuts her eyes. 'I won't say another word. I promise you, Luc, not another word.'

Empty. Mister Jack has finished the popcorn. He blows into the packet, fills it with air, dutifully squeezes the neck of the opening, then bursts the bag between his two hands with one big bang. End of programme: the young mother has left the Television Studio in tears. Fantastic programme. Now there's a commercial for a deodorant and with no transition straight into a highly clinical plug for a baby's diaper. Bravo! Slap on target. People want pathos, you serve it to them in gooey gobbets and then they clammer for more. 7247 phone calls during the programme. A record. When that dame *does* have a brat, they'll even pay for its education. What price glory! Mister Jack screws the torn packet up into a ball, shouts bang bang and aims it at the wastepaper basket. Got it, bullseye. Let's see what the old bag's doing. See-through mirror: a whopper, full to the brim! Sitting on the edge of the table, she puts her glass down and strokes her fiancé's knees. She'll get what's coming to her, that one, whatever it is. T.V., end of commercials. Here comes the Sunday evening film. Mister Jack stretches out in front of the set, a cushion at the back of his neck. He lights up a fat cigar.

He feels rich. He loves the colour of dollar bills. He closes his eyes: that is the colour he sees. He loves the sound when he's counting and re-counting his money. And what he earns from his Sunday chores is all for him, his very own. He takes a deep breath: the credits for the film, *Valley of the Dolls*. He has seen it before, but it's damned good. He finds a really soft spot in the cushion to rest his head. A cosy little nest. Like Andrew's arse.

A touch of oratory: Lucy extends a finger at Luc. 'If you only knew what goes on in the mind of a lady all alone on her way back from Lusaka and a meeting that never took place. It was like a ping-pong ball in an empty suitcase. I had nothing left. What's more, as we say in French, *"Je n'en suis pas encore revenue"*. I have never come back from Lusaka. It seems to me now that we are in a basement at the airport. And that you have seen everything and are offering to take a message for me to Barnaby and Lammert. There's still time, isn't there? I don't even know what to tell you to say. They're there, behind the door of the oven. They're going to ask you questions and you won't know what to tell them. Ah yes, say that I was wearing the green dress. They'll understand. Lammert's a good sport, he'll tip Barnaby a friendly wink. I'm sure they're working together on plans and projects. I mean, they'll not be wasting their time while they're waiting for me.' Silence. '*Maman* had gone to do the shopping.' Silence. 'I had no business opening the door while she was out.' Silence. 'And they were shouting: It's the police, open up, we're only here to protect you.' Lucy sits down next to Luc and takes his right hand in hers. 'You're not smoking, not drinking. How solemn you are! Listen, it's a terrible story. Lammert and Barnaby don't know about it. I never dared tell them. It was in the war, you know, when *Maman* had told me time and again never to open the door when she was out. I hadn't seen my father for two or three weeks. My mother told me he was away on a job but I knew she was lying. I was fifteen, working for my *Baccalauréat*. You can work it out, Luc, I shall soon be fifty. I thought the police were going to protect me. I opened the door.' Lucy squeezes Luc's hand very hard. 'So they grabbed hold of me. There were three of them. They gagged me. They told me that my mother would soon be home with her shopping, that my father would be back from his trip later on that evening, that they had a few little questions to ask them, that there was nothing to be frightened of. All I had to do was just keep still and not yell. That's all. I was to wait, with them. My mother had prepared my tea, it was on the table. They told me I could eat, but I wasn't hungry. I watched them. My mother was late. They didn't even grow impatient. They were so sure of themselves. It was then that I realised what my parents had always hidden from me. I was Jewish. But on which side? Father? Mother? I understood why my little school-mates were so envious. We had changed our name. Our name was Roussel. But my name had *always* been Lucienne Roussel. I had been baptised a Catholic, my mother had always made sure that I never missed any of my instruction in the Catechism. Then I heard my mother's steps on the stairs. From the depths of my being I screamed to her to go away. Go away, *maman*, go away! In she comes with her wicker-baskets. She doesn't look at all surprised. She comes and sits next to me and holds me very tight in her arms. Very very quietly she asks me to forgive her. She is close to tears, but fear quells everything. We wait for an hour, then another two. My father arrives. He does not seem surprised either. Briefly, we are arrested. In our first camp, near Marseilles, we are separated from my father. I never saw him again. In our third camp, near Paris, a fortnight later, my mother is taken away for interrogation. I never saw her again. When I went back home after the war, everything in the apartment had been taken, except for the chair on the balcony, because it was too old, I suppose,

210

quite shabby with the wind and the rain. I set off again, to Paris. I could only remember one address, that was my cousin Elia's.' Silence. 'There, that's what you can tell them, Luc, they never knew that. And you can add your own details if you like, to make it all seem more real, more touching, to bring tears to their eyes, if you think there's no other way to make them share your own feelings as you tell the little story of my life. Death has always been close to me.' Silence 'Now *I* can enjoy the luxury of coming close to death. So it's good to be close to you, you see, so good!'

The Valley of the Dolls, what a film, all those sex-starved dames with problems, panting to be looked after. Ah! If only I was there, thinks Mister Jack, ding, dong, and bang go all their hang-ups. Noise of bell. The old bag's ringing. Mister Jack has a peep. Lucy rings again. He shoots down the stairs four at a time, quick or he'll miss the scene where the dolls are yanking each other's hair out. He pushes open the leather door 'I was frightened, I thought you'd gone,' mumbles Lucy 'Is that all?' 'Yes. Oh and I wanted to ask you to stop the music.' 'Is that all?' 'Yes, that's all. I hope you're not waiting to go?' 'Take your time.' Mister Jack smiles, closes the door and climbs up to his office: the dolls are still at it. What a spectacle!

'It hardly seemed as if the chair on the balcony could still be the same one. A wreck of a chair. So they left it behind.' Silence. 'You won't forget, the message for Lammert and Barnaby? And remember, I don't mind you lying if you think it will please them and they want to hear a bit more. And you can tell them I couldn't send any message last time, there were too many people, and right at the end there was one fellow who didn't want to leave, he was watching me and listening to every word I said. In fact you can tell them it's not easy to have a proper tête-à-tête in this place. You'll tell them that, won't you?' Silence. 'You know, Luc, your tattoo mark reminds me of the tale about the fairy who woke up one morning with a beauty spot on the back of her left hand. She holds her hand up close to her face to have a proper look at the little black mark. Closer and closer. And as she stares at it she can make out shapes and figures, a kind of procession and bare trees in mid-winter. Closer still, and there's a snowy landscape, mourning women in black following a hearse, witches attending another witch's funeral. And the fairy is happy, for that is how she found out that her worst enemy was dead. Mother always used to tell me never to touch my beauty spots. She said they were a good omen, the mean you're going to grow more and more beautiful. Look, I've got one here.' Lucy slips the straps of her green dress down over her shoulders. 'Look, just over my breast, you see, Luc, it's very small, but I'm sure if you looked very hard you could see some extraordinary things there too.' Silence. 'Just now, when I read the word Rasky tattooed on your skin, I felt scared, you know. All of a sudden a feeling of panic. You don't mind me saying this?' Lucy stretches out and rests her head on Luc's thighs. 'You see, Luc, my face is hiding your sex. You have scars all over you, here, here and here. Poor little Luc, there wasn't much left for you and me to do on this earth, was there?' Silence. 'From down here, you look so big and strong. We were too naïve, weren't we?' Lucy shuts her eyes: the tip of her nose is against Luc's stomach. Whether she is the mother or the baby of her playmate, she is none too sure.

But what's she up to? Nothing. She's not *doing* anything. Talking, drinking, smoking, sitting close to him, touching him with her fingertips, standing up and walking round the low table, sitting down again, rambling on and on. Mister Jack, hands in pockets, cigar stuck in his mouth, has just turned off the T.V. a few minutes before the end of the film: the screams of those Hollywood dolls were getting on his nerves. The see-through mirror: he watches

212

and waits. If only the old bag would take her dress off, a least it would pass the time, a little indecency. Not even that. Has she gone to sleep? No, she's getting up, taking hold of the body by the shoulders, trying to lay it flat on the couch. The knees won't bend. She presses down on them and pulls the arms out straight. The two straps of her dress have slipped off and part of her breast is visible. Mister Jack goes to his desk-drawer to fetch his binoculars. That's right, not wearing a bra, not bad for her age. Hey there! Something's going to happen. She is stroking the body from head to foot and back again, running her hands through the hair, arranging her little boy's hair, lifting the back of his neck and setting the hair back in place. Then she closes Luc's eyes and slowly, very slowly, removes her dress. It falls to the ground: she lies down on the couch beside Luc, tight up against him. Lays her head on his shoulder: she is a little shorter than he is. Where are her hands? Mister Jack can no longer see the old bag's hands. He can only see Lucy's back concealing a part of Luc's body. He is trying to see her hands: no hands. Pity. All far too *nice*. Mister Jack goes and puts his binoculars away in the drawer and stamps out the butt of his cigar in a heart-shaped ashtray. He feels the same about the ashtray as he does about that sofa and the coffee table: he loathes it. He chucks it in the wastepaper basket. Paces round the office. Looks at his watch. Half past eleven. Patience, patience!

'Are you taking me with you, Luc? Take me with you. Show me the way.' Lucy has lifted her face to Luc's. She whispers very very softly into his ear. 'I'm quite serious, you know, but I'm not sure how to go about it. I've never been summoned. My father and my mother, yes, but not me, ever. I must have been forgotten. Or perhaps they think I'm over-anxious. Come on, answer!' Lucy nibbles at Luc's ear, presses Luc's left hand between hers, against her genitals, and flattens herself against the prostrate body, which supports and transports her, as a chill runs right through her. 'Answer me!'

213

Mister Jack has had enough. Twenty to twelve. It's gone on far too long. He switches on the crematorium. He'll give the old bag a fright. In three minutes it will be ready. The old crone will be let off with a caution. Mister Jack giggles. When he tells his buddies about it, later on, if he ever *does* give the story away, nobody will believe him. The Sicilian will call him *sorpasso* and with a shrug of the shoulders hand him a cigar. Mister Jack dives for his binoculars again: he wants a close-up of this. Great! The crematorium's ready. He presses the red button. The gate behind the podium opens and the podium glides toward it with its tableau complete: couch, low table, green dress and the two of them in a clinch. 'Shit, she hasn't moved.' Mister Jack holds his breath. 'Jump!' The old bag doesn't move. 'JUMP, FOR CHRISSAKE!' The podium vanishes into the oven and the gate closes. All over.

Mister Jack drops his binoculars, which strike the floor with an ugly thud. Scared out of his wits, he titters and clings with his palms to the see-through mirror. It has all happened so fast! And he could never have dreamed that . . . SHIT! He bursts out laughing, and that's a help. He spins round in circles, clasping his head in his hands, shouting. 'She went in, she went in!'

Lucy just had the time to bite Luc's ear very hard, in order to screw up her courage.

Mister Jack tears down the stairs, flings the leather door open, upsets the benches in the chapel and rushes to the end of the room. He consults his watch: two minutes more. He hammers on the wall with his fists. He is crazy with fear. And dancing with joy. That's what he calls a show! And Madam Lucy will never telephone him again. Yippeeee! Nine hundred bucks. The green light appears over the door. Mister Jack presses the Return button. The podium reappears with the ashes, the charred remains. Ten minutes to midnight: nothing left to do but clean up. What the eye doesn't see . . .

214

'Hey, Lucio, I guess I'm gonna make holes in the pockets of *all* my pants.'

Chapter Thirty-Nine

Andrew is pacing up and down in front of the chapel. He turns his back to the wind, hunches his shoulders to keep warm and aims a few kicks at the curb. The passing cabs slow down, but he waves them on with a sign that he is waiting. And when a pedestrian eyes him too insistently, he switches sidewalks. Mister Jack finally emerges. Andrew runs up to him. 'Well, Lily, what are you doing here?' 'I wanna know. Everything come off O.K.?' 'Sure, everything come off fine.' 'What've you got in that packet?' 'You guess.' Mister Jack is smiling. 'Come on, better not hang around. Let's walk.' At the corner of Columbus Avenue, Andrew swings to a halt in front of Mister Jack. 'What've you got in that brown paper bag?' 'What d'you think I've got? Your little buddy's ashes. Conscience bothering you?' Silence. Andrew shrugs his shoulders and kicks the tyre of a parked car. 'What's the matter then, what's bugging you?' Mister Jack holds the packet out in front of him. 'You wanna taste?' Andrew throws himself at Mister Jack and grips him by the collar of his shirt. The packet falls to the ground and bursts open. 'Hey, man! Back off! Maybe you want a taste of the joint. A nice long stretch. It's black as hell in there, so you wouldn't show. The pokey, just tell me, is that what you want?' Andrew lets go. Mister Jack grips him by the shoulder. 'Come on, pick 'em all up, I've just spent the last hour cleaning my place. Now move, it's your turn!' Andrew goes down on his knees and collects the ashes. 'The bag's busted. Take your jacket off and stuff all that inside. I'll teach you to play the Queen of Sheba. It's a bit late, Lily, for this hearts and flowers crap.' Silence. 'I get it, Lily spends all day sleeping and when she opens her big round eyes, she starts wondering what she got up to last night. Madam has a fit of remorse. Can you beat that? Here, give that to me.' Mister Jack takes the rolled-up jacket, slips it under one arm and calls a cab. 'Go and rest up good, beauty, and tomorrow you can sell all those pretty cut flowers, as if nothing ever happened.' He opens the cab door. 'And next time you call me up, I won't forget who messed up my shirt.' Andrew, with bared arms, his head sunk in his shoulders, steps back, and then takes to his heels. The cab pulls away. Mister Jack is going home, with his two babies on his lap.

Chapter Forty

Columbus Day. The Parade. Every school in New York City is in the procession. Drum-majorettes, pompoms, satins of every hue, whistles blowing, brass bands playing drums and flags, standards bearing the arms of the New World's Cardinals, and chestnuts, hot chestnuts: the pretzel-vendors are selling the first chestnuts of the year. A cold wind sharpens the sound and colour of the celebrations. Kenneth asks the night porter if Madam Lucy is back. 'No.' 'That's funny.' And that is all. The roads in Central Park are closed to vehicles. Mister Jack has rented a bicycle at the corner of 77th Street and 2nd Avenue. He has placed the paper bag in the small basket in front of the handlebars. He cycles up 77th Street to Central Park. He is off for a nice little ride. A real breath of fresh air with some exercise thrown in. He'll go round the Reservoir on the cinder track which is prohibited to cyclists, but what the hell. He likes this great lake imprisoned by a wire fence and the silhouette of Manhattan against the sky reflected on the surface of the water: 'It's the best-looking thing in this fucking city.' He pedals along slowly. Various strollers point out to him that cyclists are not allowed there. He just carries on. Every now and then he bends over the paper bag and takes out a few ashes, which he scatters over the track. They will get crushed and trodden in by the walkers and runners who turn out on Sundays, those dead days when everyone kills time. Mister Jack will go right round the Reservoir. He husbands his reserves: he must complete the circuit. To make a fine necklace of ashes for New York City. And he alone will know the secret of its existence. That amuses him.

219

The circuit is complete. Mister Jack dismounts. There are still a few ashes left at the bottom of the bag. He forces his way through the bushes until he comes to an avenue. He walks along to the Fountain and buys himself a coke. Round the Fountain another parade is in progress, beribboned dogs, and cats being taken for a ride in baskets on wheels, the parade of motley footwear, extravagant platform shoes, denim slacks and skirts sporting constellations of embroidered butterflies. Peace, Sex, Orgasm, Hell's Angel, various devices. Mister Jack climbs back on his bicycle and looks out for a quiet corner, a grassy bank among the bushes. He leans his bicycle against the bank and sits down with the bag in his lap. He calls the squirrels. Ptt! Ptt! Here they come, one, two, three. He throws the last of the ashes in their direction, some distance away among the grass, at the foot of the trees. The squirrels approach the titbits, take them in their paws, start to nibble them, then reject them. When the bag is empty, Mister Jack blows into it, squeezes it round the neck and bursts it with both hands. Bang.

Full stop. The more phantoms I kill, the more there are. Adventure is dead.

THE END

SELECTED DALKEY ARCHIVE PAPERBACKS

PETROS ABATZOGLOU, *What Does Mrs. Freeman Want?*
PIERRE ALBERT-BIROT, *Grabinoulor.*
YUZ ALESHKOVSKY, *Kangaroo.*
FELIPE ALFAU, *Chromos.*
  Locos.
IVAN ÂNGELO, *The Celebration.*
  The Tower of Glass.
DAVID ANTIN, *Talking.*
DJUNA BARNES, *Ladies Almanack.*
  Ryder.
JOHN BARTH, *LETTERS.*
  Sabbatical.
DONALD BARTHELME, *The King.*
  Paradise.
SVETISLAV BASARA, *Chinese Letter.*
MARK BINELLI, *Sacco and Vanzetti Must Die!*
ANDREI BITOV, *Pushkin House.*
LOUIS PAUL BOON, *Chapel Road.*
  Summer in Termuren.
ROGER BOYLAN, *Killoyle.*
IGNÁCIO DE LOYOLA BRANDÃO, *Zero.*
CHRISTINE BROOKE-ROSE, *Amalgamemnon.*
BRIGID BROPHY, *In Transit.*
MEREDITH BROSNAN, *Mr. Dynamite.*
GERALD L. BRUNS,
  Modern Poetry and the Idea of Language.
GABRIELLE BURTON, *Heartbreak Hotel.*
MICHEL BUTOR, *Degrees.*
  Mobile.
  Portrait of the Artist as a Young Ape.
G. CABRERA INFANTE, *Infante's Inferno.*
  Three Trapped Tigers.
JULIETA CAMPOS, *The Fear of Losing Eurydice.*
ANNE CARSON, *Eros the Bittersweet.*
CAMILO JOSÉ CELA, *The Family of Pascual Duarte.*
  The Hive.
LOUIS-FERDINAND CÉLINE, *Castle to Castle.*
  Conversations with Professor Y.
  London Bridge.
  North.
  Rigadoon.
HUGO CHARTERIS, *The Tide Is Right.*
JEROME CHARYN, *The Tar Baby.*
MARC CHOLODENKO, *Mordechai Schamz.*
EMILY HOLMES COLEMAN, *The Shutter of Snow.*
ROBERT COOVER, *A Night at the Movies.*
STANLEY CRAWFORD, *Some Instructions to My Wife.*
ROBERT CREELEY, *Collected Prose.*
RENÉ CREVEL, *Putting My Foot in It.*
RALPH CUSACK, *Cadenza.*
SUSAN DAITCH, *L.C.*
  Storytown.
NIGEL DENNIS, *Cards of Identity.*
PETER DIMOCK,
  A Short Rhetoric for Leaving the Family.
ARIEL DORFMAN, *Konfidenz.*
COLEMAN DOWELL, *The Houses of Children.*
  Island People.
  Too Much Flesh and Jabez.
RIKKI DUCORNET, *The Complete Butcher's Tales.*
  The Fountains of Neptune.
  The Jade Cabinet.
  Phosphor in Dreamland.
  The Stain.
  The Word "Desire."
WILLIAM EASTLAKE, *The Bamboo Bed.*
  Castle Keep.
  Lyric of the Circle Heart.
JEAN ECHENOZ, *Chopin's Move.*
STANLEY ELKIN, *A Bad Man.*
  Boswell: A Modern Comedy.
  Criers and Kibitzers, Kibitzers and Criers.
  The Dick Gibson Show.
  The Franchiser.
  George Mills.
  The Living End.
  The MacGuffin.
  The Magic Kingdom.

  Mrs. Ted Bliss.
  The Rabbi of Lud.
  Van Gogh's Room at Arles.
ANNIE ERNAUX, *Cleaned Out.*
LAUREN FAIRBANKS, *Muzzle Thyself.*
  Sister Carrie.
LESLIE A. FIEDLER,
  Love and Death in the American Novel.
GUSTAVE FLAUBERT, *Bouvard and Pécuchet.*
FORD MADOX FORD, *The March of Literature.*
CARLOS FUENTES, *Christopher Unborn.*
  Distant Relations.
  Terra Nostra.
  Where the Air Is Clear.
JANICE GALLOWAY, *Foreign Parts.*
  The Trick Is to Keep Breathing.
WILLIAM H. GASS, *The Tunnel.*
  Willie Masters' Lonesome Wife.
ETIENNE GILSON, *The Arts of the Beautiful.*
  Forms and Substances in the Arts.
C. S. GISCOMBE, *Giscome Road.*
  Here.
DOUGLAS GLOVER, *Bad News of the Heart.*
  The Enamoured Knight.
KAREN ELIZABETH GORDON, *The Red Shoes.*
GEORGI GOSPODINOV, *Natural Novel.*
PATRICK GRAINVILLE, *The Cave of Heaven.*
HENRY GREEN, *Blindness.*
  Concluding.
  Doting.
  Nothing.
JIŘÍ GRUŠA, *The Questionnaire.*
JOHN HAWKES, *Whistlejacket.*
AIDAN HIGGINS, *A Bestiary.*
  Bornholm Night-Ferry.
  Flotsam and Jetsam.
  Langrishe, Go Down.
  Scenes from a Receding Past.
  Windy Arbours.
ALDOUS HUXLEY, *Antic Hay.*
  Crome Yellow.
  Point Counter Point.
  Those Barren Leaves.
  Time Must Have a Stop.
MIKHAIL IOSSEL and JEFF PARKER, EDS., *Amerika:*
  Contemporary Russians View
  the United States.
GERT JONKE, *Geometric Regional Novel.*
JACQUES JOUET, *Mountain R.*
HUGH KENNER, *The Counterfeiters.*
  Flaubert, Joyce and Beckett:
  The Stoic Comedians.
DANILO KIŠ, *Garden, Ashes.*
  A Tomb for Boris Davidovich.
ANITA KONKKA, *A Fool's Paradise.*
TADEUSZ KONWICKI, *A Minor Apocalypse.*
  The Polish Complex.
MENIS KOUMANDAREAS, *Koula.*
ELAINE KRAF, *The Princess of 72nd Street.*
JIM KRUSOE, *Iceland.*
EWA KURYLUK, *Century 21.*
VIOLETTE LEDUC, *La Bâtarde.*
DEBORAH LEVY, *Billy and Girl.*
  Pillow Talk in Europe and Other Places.
JOSÉ LEZAMA LIMA, *Paradiso.*
OSMAN LINS, *Avalovara.*
  The Queen of the Prisons of Greece.
ALF MAC LOCHLAINN, *The Corpus in the Library.*
  Out of Focus.
RON LOEWINSOHN, *Magnetic Field(s).*
D. KEITH MANO, *Take Five.*
BEN MARCUS, *The Age of Wire and String.*
WALLACE MARKFIELD, *Teitlebaum's Window.*
  To an Early Grave.
DAVID MARKSON, *Reader's Block.*
  Springer's Progress.
  Wittgenstein's Mistress.

FOR A FULL LIST OF PUBLICATIONS, VISIT:
www.dalkeyarchive.com

SELECTED DALKEY ARCHIVE PAPERBACKS

FOR A FULL LIST OF PUBLICATIONS, VISIT:
www.dalkeyarchive.com